The Avengers of San Pedro

Renegades raid San Pedro, a small Mexican settlement near one of the largest ranches in Texas, massacring most of its inhabitants. Seeking to avenge the massacre, Brad Miller pursues the renegades across the Texas border into New Mexico. But a dreadful storm forces him to seek shelter in a small and isolated ranch owned by Jane Latham.

Brad soon discovers he is caught in the the middle of a feud between the Bar Zero ranch and the Blackwash Silver Mine. By helping Jane, Brad is caught up in the feud, but finds the renegades are also involved.

As range war breaks out, Brad is forced to enlist the aid of a deadly gunman also pursuing the renegades. Together, they must bring justice to New Mexico, where the only law is the six-gun.

The Avengers of San Pedro

EDWIN DEREK

A Black Horse Western

ROBERT HALE · LONDON

ISBN 978-0-7090-8675-8

Robert Hale Limited
Clerkenwell House
Clerkenwell Green
London EC1R 0HT

www.halebooks.com

Typeset by
Derek Doyle & Associates, Shaw Heath
Printed and bound in Great Britain by
CPI Antony Rowe, Wiltshire

CHAPTER ONE

The sky was as black as ink although it was at least an hour until sunset. Stinging hail, driven by the storm-force wind, lashed down. Brad's horse whinnied nervously as thunder echoed ominously in the nearby hills. Lightning briefly lit up the sky, but thankfully, the centre of the storm was still some distance away.

Driven by the howling wind, the hail cut into his face. Thankfully, it soon turned to torrential rain. But within a few seconds, Brad was soaking wet and shivering with cold. This was the first time he had ridden so far West and the ferocity of the storm had caught him completely unprepared.

Brad was on the trail of a gang of renegades who had killed almost everybody in a small and isolated settlement called San Pedro. Its people, mainly

Mexican, were unarmed because they were under the protection of the nearby Double M, one of the largest ranches in Texas.

Unfortunately, a serious outbreak of rustling on the opposite side of the ranch to the San Pedro settlement meant that it had been left unprotected. And that was when the renegades struck.

Strangely, the renegades had left a young Mexican girl alive to identify the gang and relate her terrible ordeal. Three renegades had raped her in front of her mortally wounded husband, a young American called Seth Madden. As they performed their vile act, their leader repeatedly called out their names and incited them to further acts of bestiality. The three gang members involved were Frank Tucker, 'Reb' Rosin and a gunman called Spite. They were known to be part of Nate Killner's outlaw gang wanted for robbery and murder in Kansas and Texas.

Although he was only twenty-one years old, Seth Madden had already featured on several wanted posters. Like many before him, he had drifted into bad company and hit the outlaw trail. Yet, once freed from their influence, he was a decent enough lad and had tried to go straight. Perhaps it was the love of a beautiful woman that had made him want to settle down. So the Double M had decided to give him that chance and had given him a job as wrangler in spite of a $500 dollar reward for his capture, dead or alive.

However, Brad could not believe that the reward had been the renegades' motive for killing Seth. Not only had they had ridden off without trying to claim it, they had also killed many innocent and unarmed Mexicans.

The renegades' motive for attacking San Pedro was a complete mystery. Robbery could not have been the reason. The Mexican inhabitants were either poor dirt farmers or worked as dollar-a-day cowboys on Double M. But how did the renegades know the settlement was undefended and why had they left the girl alive to tell the world who had raped her and carried out the massacre? To find the answers to these riddles and to avenge the good folk of San Pedro, Brad had taken leave of absence from the Double M and followed the trail left by the outlaws.

One of the renegades' horses had a curious v-shaped grove in its front right hoof. Surprisingly, its owner had not changed the horse or had it reshod. In fact, the renegades had made little attempt to hide their trail, so Brad was able to follow them as they rode out of Texas into New Mexico.

That had been some time ago. Now, the

violence of the storm had washed away the rene-gades' trail. In fact, Brad was lost. He could only guess he was somewhere near the Arizona border. But if that was so, neither the heavily wooded land-scape nor the inclement weather was anything like the arid semi-desert his fellow Texans had told him to expect.

There was no way Brad could outrun the storm. His horse, Prince, had thrown a shoe. Indeed, if it had not been for the thunder and lightning, Brad would have dismounted and led the stallion, cavalry style, towards any shelter he could find. But Prince was too spooked to be held by his reins. So there was no alternative, he had to ride on. However, he guessed that Killner's gang would seek shelter from the storm, so with every limping stride of his gallant horse, he was be gaining on them.

Brad knew the renegades were headed to Blackwater. With the aid of the v-groove, Brad had been able to track them to a small settlement near El Capitan Mountain. Surprisingly, they had not been shy in disclosing their names when they bought fresh supplies. Indeed, they had even told the storekeeper they were headed for a town called Blackwater. It almost seemed as if they wanted to be followed.

As the rain became even stronger, the two full

canteens of water Brad had been advised to carry seemed a mite superfluous. Again lightning flashed across the sky, but this time it was nearer and the thunder was even louder. He could almost feel the panic in his horse.

Prince had reason to be scared. Brad was only too aware that lightning seemed to be strangely attracted to a solitary rider unfortunate enough to be caught out in the vast open expanses of the West. So he had to find shelter before the lightning found him.

Another bolt lit up the indigo sky, and struck the ground with a frightening roar. This time, it was near enough to cause the panic-stricken horse to rear and Brad had to keep the beast under control. But at least the lightning temporarily lit up was left of the trail and Brad could see it split into two.

The rain had washed out all signs of tracks on the main trail but he could still detect some signs on the side-trail. These had made by the wheels of a heavily laden wagon. One track wobbled badly, indicating the rear, left-hand side wheel was dangerously loose, so loose that it was clear that the wagon could not have travelled much further. Therefore, he guessed that there might a ranch or homestead not too far down the side trail.

There was. The wobbly wagon tracks led directly

to a small ranch house, or was it a larger than usual homestead? Whichever, Brad reached it just in time. The worst of the violent storm was now almost directly overhead, scaring Prince out of the few wits he possessed.

Smoke coming from the chimney of the ranch house indicated that it was occupied, although there was no other sign of life. Brad looked around for somewhere to stable Prince, but the fence of the ranch's empty corral was broken, rendering it useless. Fortunately, there was a barn nearby and its door had been left ajar. On closer inspection, the door was also in need of repair and could not be fully closed. But any port in a storm, thought Brad, as he led Prince into the barn's gloomy interior.

They were met by the frightened neigh of a terrified horse. Much to Brad's dismay, the huge beast was still harnessed to an ancient wagon laden with rough-sawn timber. Presumably the timber was to rebuild the corral and repair the barn door, but the load had proved too much for the old wagon. Although its back wheel was still attached, it slanted outwards at a crazy angle, accounting for the wobbly tracks he had followed. Timber must have come from a sawmill. So was there a town nearby? Was it Blackwater? Even if it wasn't, the renegades might have stopped to shelter there.

Brad decided to ride on as soon as the storm had died down and find out.

Providing, of course, Prince could carry him. Unfortunately, the interior of the barn was far too dark to examine Prince's leg. So, instead, Brad unharnessed the terrified carthorse from its wagon and tethered it to a hitching rail which, unusually, had been built inside the barn.

Brad looked round the barn's gloomy interior. Apart from the wagon, several lengths of rope, a few cans of paint and a small quantity of hay, it was surprisingly empty. However, as he looked upwards into the murky gloom of the barn's roof, he spied a wagon wheel lashed to the rafters.

Brad could not close the broken barn door unaided, so he hitched the still terror stricken Prince next to the other horse. However, as both horses were in a state of panic, he picked up a length of rope and expertly formed it into what the Easterners called a lasso, a term seldom used by true Texas cowboys who confusingly called the lasso a rope. He used it to hobble the forelegs of Prince and then used a separate rope to hobble the other horse. He didn't want either of them to rear in panic and smash their forelegs into each other.

Both horses needed rubbing down, but the likelihood of the horses being spooked by lightning or

11

thunder made the job too dangerous. Besides, Brad was wet and cold and the smoke coming from the ranch-house chimney indicated that there was a warm fire underneath it. The code of the West meant that if he paid a call, he should be invited into the ranch-house.

After careful deliberation, Brad decided to leave his Winchester carbine in the barn. He did not want to provoke or scare the occupants of the ranch house into a rash shot. As events were to turn out, this seemingly unimportant decision was destined to set into motion a series of events which were to change the rest of Brad's life.

As he hurried across the courtyard to the little ranch house, his star-shaped, work-spurs jangled over the noise of the storm. But he was drenched again by the time he reached the ranch-house door because the reinforced arches and tall heels of his cowboy boots were made for riding, not running.

Lightning flashed overhead, but this time there was no thunder. Instead, the roaring wind reached little short of hurricane strength and almost blew him over. Ice-cold rain lashed brutally into his face making him wish he was back in the comparative safety of his Texas home.

He rapped on the door. After what seemed an age, it was unbolted. Framed by the flickering flames of a welcoming fire was a young woman. But she didn't seem friendly for she held a cocked six-gun, pointed at Brad's chest.

CHAPTER TWO

The six-gun remained steady. It was a Navy Colt, but at such close range its small .38 calibre bullet could be as deadly the .45 fired by Brad's new Peacemaker.

'Ma'am, my horse is lame, so I need shelter.' Brad had to shout to be heard over the raging storm.

The woman beckoned Brad into a surprisingly large and well-kept room. All of its oak window-shutters were closed and secured firmly by stout bars. The room was lit by a single oil lamp augmented by the flames of a log fire, and alto-gether the room gave out a warm and friendly feel-ing. The feeling was heightened by the delightful aroma of cooking emanating from the kitchen. Its delicious smell reminded him he had not eaten that day.

'Close the door and bolt it,' ordered the woman,

keeping her old six-gun pointed straight at Brad.

He complied with her orders without protest. But his clothes were so wet, his slightest movement sent streams of water cascading on to the polished oak floor. However, the woman seemed unconcerned at his plight.

'Unbuckle your gunbelt,' she ordered. 'You can stay for the duration of the storm, even if you are one of Jed Hawker's new gunmen. But one false move and I will shoot to kill!'

'Understood, ma'am, but you've nothing to fear from me. You have my word as a Texan. I was just riding through when my horse went lame, so I got caught in the storm.'

As he spoke, Brad slowly unbuckled his gunbelt and gently lowered it to the floor. Although she had not so instructed, he kicked it over to her. Even so, she was still not satisfied.

'If you're riding through, where's your horse?'

'Took the liberty of putting him in your barn, ma'am, before coming to the house. Although Prince is lame, he's too skittish to rub down; I guess he doesn't like this storm any more than I do.'

'What about my horse?' she asked sharply.

'Took another liberty there, ma' am, and unharnessed him. He and my horse Prince are both tethered and safely hobbled.'

The woman smiled briefly, but her attitude remained unchanged it seemed. As Brad stood in front of the now bolted front door, water from his saturated clothes still continued to pour on to the floor to form an ever growing pool. He felt like a drowned rat.

'I thank you for unharnessing my horse. Normally the big fellow is as quiet as a mouse, but I guess the storm got to him and made him wild. Unfortunately, I'm not that experienced with horses and he was too lively for me to handle.'

'No trouble, ma'am,' said Brad beginning to relax. As he did so he slightly lowered his hands.

'Keep your hands raised,' the woman snapped. 'If you lower them another inch, I'll fill you full of holes. Do you understand?'

'Yes, ma'am. I won't move. But you've nothing to fear from me. I swear that I've never heard of this Jed Hawker you just mentioned.'

The rain must have turned back to hail for Brad could hear the wind driving it into the shutters. Then, much to his surprise, the woman suddenly retreated into the kitchen. However, she was only gone for an instant. She returned carrying a large pink towel in her left hand and threw it on to the floor by his feet. However, she still held a six-gun in her other hand and continued to point it at Brad.

'Strip off your boots and clothes, then dry yourself,' she ordered.

'But, ma'am!'

Brad began to protest but it was no use. She had the gun and it was still cocked. His struggle to keep his body hidden behind the towel as he stripped caused her much merriment. But, in spite of his embarrassment, Brad found the sound of her gentle laughter quite pleasant.

She bent down, picked up his gunbelt, and then took it into the kitchen. This time when she returned she carried a fluffy, pink dressing-gown. Much to Brad's further embarrassment, she made him put it on. Again, he could not argue, for her Navy Colt was still pointing at him. She then picked up his clothes and again retreated back into the kitchen. This time, when she returned, she carried a bowl of hot stew instead of the old six-gun.

'You don't look quite so ornery just wearing your hat and my dressing-gown,' she said, smiling. She put the stew on the table and beckoned Brad to sit down.

Her face lit up as she did so, softening her appearance, made to look unnecessarily severe by the tight bun at the back of her head into which her hair had been curled.

While he was eating, Brad studied her face. She was not a classic beauty. Her chin was a little too determined and her cheeks just a little too broad for that. Nevertheless, there was something about her that instantly set her aside from any other woman he had ever met. Although she wore a simple cornflower blue gingham dress, it could not hide the near perfection of her body. Indeed, in the flickering light of the oil lamp, she looked nothing like his image of a homesteader's wife. Then he noticed she was not wearing a ring.

'Finished looking me over?' she asked sharply.

He hadn't realized he had been staring.

'Sorry, ma'am. No offence meant. You don't fit my idea of a homesteader.'

'This is a ranch not a homestead, and dressed in my old pink dressing-gown, you don't fit my idea of a gunman,' she said drily. 'But do stop calling me, ma'am: my name is Jane Latham.'

'I'm Bradley Miller. My friends call me Brad, Miss Latham.'

'Well, you're hardly dressed for formality, but I shall call you Mr Miller until you call me Jane.'

'Yes, ma'am, I mean, Jane. Thanks for the stew, it was delicious. It sure warmed me up.'

'Just rabbit and a few vegetables and herbs,' she said modestly. 'I'm afraid I'm a bit short of provisions at the moment.'

'I noticed your barn is almost empty, but surely you're not here in this wilderness on your own?'

18

asked Brad remembering she had said the big cart-horse was too spooked for her to unharness.

A look of apprehension passed across her face, telling him he had guessed correctly. He spoke quietly to reassure her.

'I know I'm a stranger to you, but I gave you my word, so you are quite safe.'

'I begin to believe that I may be, but I'm not usually alone, something or somebody has driven my men and my Indians into the hills.'

'Your Indians?' replied Brad in surprise. 'I thought this part of the world was home to the Comanche.'

'Apache not Comanche. But in any case, they haven't bothered me since I settled here,' Jane replied. 'No, my Indians are the Yampai. They are very timid and primitive people, nothing like the Apache.'

'Yampai? I don't think I've ever heard of that tribe,' said Brad.

'Nor had I until I came here,' replied Jane.

Brad found talking to her was surprisingly easy and gradually began to feel at ease, in spite of the garment he was wearing. He learnt that she had been born in New England where she had been a schoolteacher. Unfortunately, her father had contracted consumption; ironically, he had been a doctor. They had chosen to come West in the belief that the warmer and drier climate would help him recover.

Although the climate, especially in winter, had been much warmer than in New England, this part of New Mexico hadn't been quite as dry as they had expected. Nevertheless, initially all had gone well and they settled in what was then the quiet little town of Blackwater. But soon after they had moved in, silver had been discovered in the nearby hills.

Jane said that at first the discovery of silver was good news. The sudden influx of miners led to an urgent need for a doctor, first in the mining camp and then in Blackwater. But the miners kept on arriving and with them came gunmen and gamblers. Unfortunately, the once quiet little town rapidly became a lawless den of iniquity.

And yet this did not deter the arrival of more and more miners. Soon there were too many for Blackwater to accommodate. So the company which had appeared out of nowhere and taken control of the mine, established a permanent camp within easy walking distance from the mine entrance and a little over two hours' ride from Blackwater.

At first, most of the miners stayed put, only visiting the town at weekends and they contented themselves with getting drunk. However, trouble flared between them and the local cowboys, and the miners usually fared worse. Although patching up the injured miners provided more work for Jane's father, the trouble had serious repercussions; the mining company began to hire gunmen to protect their men.

The tables were turned on the cowboys until the Bar Zero, by far the largest and most powerful ranch in the area, also began to employ gunmen. Unfortunately, the situation worsened as several more saloons opened in Blackwater. In them, prostitutes vied with gamblers to relieve the miners and cowboys of their hard-earned money.

Apart from the shootings in Blackwater's saloons, accidents at the silver mine were frequent. So her father was all too often called out. As a result, his health began to decline. However, the miners paid well and he was soon able to purchase a small but unprofitable ranch. For that reason, it had been called the Little Use.

Sadly, the decline in Jane's father's health continued apace. The New Mexican climate, instead of curing him, merely postponed the inevitable and he died from consumption before he could move into the ranch.

Typically, just before died, Dr Latham befriended and treated for free, several local Indians from the Yampai tribe. He even travelled into the nearby hills to deliver the baby of the chief's wife. So, when Jane eventually moved into the ranch, a few of them began to do chores for her. She also changed the name of the ranch to the Little U, which was a rough translation of the name given to the baby of the Yampai chief.

Jane kept the next part of her life story to herself. The ranch which was in poor condition, deteriorated still further before she could move in. Unfortunately, her father, never good with money, had spent most of his earnings and the salary she earned as a schoolteacher was only just enough to live on.

However, there had been and still was a huge demand for saloon girls, especially as pretty as Jane. Few of the miners or cowhands who patronized the Lucky Strike cared that Jane's singing voice was less than perfect. Quite the opposite, for to compensate, her dresses were so revealing, the former schoolteacher soon became the toast of Blackwater. In less than a year, she made enough money to begin to rebuild the Little U and hire a couple of hands to help run it.

But Jane didn't tell Brad how she had raised the money. Instead, she told him how her hired help had departed although the work was barely half done. Since then, she had been unable to hire anybody else.

But she had already paid for the timber to rebuild the barn door and the corral, so with the help of several miners who remembered her daring performances at the Lucky Strike Saloon, the timber was loaded onto her old wagon. The load had almost been too heavy for it and she only just made it back to her barn. That had been just as the storm broke, barely an hour before Brad had knocked on the ranch-house door.

As she talked, time seemed to fly by, even if the storm did not. When she retired, it was almost midnight and still raining as hard as ever. Brad bunked down on the large couch in the main room.

CHAPTER THREE

Brad slept soundly. After weeks on the trail, sleeping rough, the couch was a luxury not a hardship. He awoke to find that his boots had been cleaned and were on the floor beside him. However, there was no sign of the rest of his clothes, or his new Colt Peacemaker.

Dawn was just beginning to break. It seemed the storm had abated. Brad put on his boots and, clad only in the pink dressing-gown and his hat, quietly slipped outside. Everywhere was covered in deep puddles but the rising sun revealed a cloudless sky, Although the wind had died down to a whisper, it was still surprisingly cold.

Brad made his way to the barn, hoping he did not look as ridiculous as he felt. Luckily, it seemed that Jane's Indians had not returned for there was nobody about. As he reached the barn, he was greeted by welcoming neighs from Prince and Jane's cart-horse. Now that the storm had passed, they were both back to normal, so Brad removed the hobbling ropes from their forelegs.

Next, Brad hurried to his saddle-bags and pulled out the spare set of clothes he always carried and quickly put them on. Then, he carefully examined Prince. The horse had cast a shoe and there was severe bruising above the unshod hoof. But it didn't look too serious. After few days' rest in the barn, Prince should be fine. However, that meant the trip into Blackwater and a visit to its blacksmith would have to be delayed.

Using some of the hay stacked in the corner of the barn, Brad fed the horses. Whilst they were greedily feeding, he examined the wagon. The rear wheel was damaged beyond repair. However, with a little bit of ingenuity, it could be replaced by the one lashed to the rafters. But first, he would have to unload the timber.

Before he could remove the broken wheel, he would have to connect one end of his rope to the rear axle of the wagon and then run the rope over the block and pulley fixed to one of the main roof beams. The other end of the rope would have to be attached to the cart-horse. As it walked out of the barn, the rope would tighten and lift the rear of the wagon off the ground and that would allow him to remove the damaged wheel and replace it with the spare. Finally, the cart-horse would walk back to the wagon, thus releasing the tension on the rope. The wagon should then drop back to the floor, almost as good as new.

But first, the horses had to be groomed. As his thoughts turned to getting the wagon wheel down, the sound of approaching riders interrupted his deliberations. At first, Brad thought it was none of his business and continued to groom Prince. However, when he heard Jane's voice raised in anger, he decided it was time to make it his business. Reaching for the Winchester carbine he had left in the barn the night before, he slipped silently outside. Two riders had dismounted and one of them was giving Jane a hard time.

'My boss, Mr Hawker, thinks it ain't fitting for a single lady to live out here on her own. He says he has had a long chat with your mangy Indians, so is certain that they will not be back to keep you company.'

Apart from the pearl-handles of his two six-guns, the speaker was dressed completely in black. However, he was not wearing chaps, essential leg protection for any cowboy or drover, so Brad concluded the man was a professional gun-slinger.

The second man was wearing chaps and his clothes looked trail-worn. Although his gun-rig also had two holsters, they were entirely different in style. Only the left-hand one, cut down for a quicker draw, revealed a six-gun. Strangely, its frame appeared to be almost yellow in the early morning light.

The one for the rider's right-hand looked like an old cavalry-style holster complete with a flap on top of it. As the flap was firmly tied down, Brad could not detect what sort of six-gun made it bulge out, but wrongly assumed it must be an old Dragoon Colt, perhaps the largest handgun made by Sam Colt's men. To complete his armament, the rider also carried a Bowie knife in a shoulder rig.

'Miss Jane,' said the second rider politely, 'changing the name of your ranch from the Little Use to the Little U won't make it any more success-ful. As a ranch, it is really too small to be much good, so I'm afraid it's still of *little use*!'

Both gunmen were so busy laughing at the play on words, neither noticed Brad approach. For the moment, he paused and listened, as the flashily dressed gunslinger continued to talk to Jane.

'My new friend from Texas is right,' said the flashily dressed gunman. 'So why not be sensible and sell? My boss, Mr Hawker, will pay enough for you to go back East and still have enough to start teaching again. Why, for your safety, he might arrange for me or my friend to ride guard on your stagecoach!'

'Miss Jane, this country is too wild and dangerous for a woman on her own,' said the second rider, 'I'd sure hate for you to have an accident out here.'

'So would I,' said Brad, carbine in hand. He had stopped, quite deliberately, about thirty-five paces away from them. 'Are these men bothering you, ma'am?'

'Who the hell are you?' asked the gunman dressed in black before Jane could reply.

'The man with a Winchester,' replied Brad quietly. 'Now if you've had your say, there's nothing to keep you here, so I'll bid you good day.'

Had he taken the carbine to the house instead of leaving it in the barn, Jane would have undoubtedly taken possession of it last night. Consequently, this morning, he would have been unable to make the intervention which was to affect the rest of his life.

But at that moment there was nothing to suggest this, nor was there anything threatening in Brad's

28

words. It was just that he was standing just too far away from the gunmen for them to get an accurate shot from their six-guns. However, for a Winchester carbine, thirty-five or so paces was point-blank range.

'Stranger, I don't take kindly to you interfering in matters that don't concern you,' said the gunslinger dressed in black.

'You just made them my business and, as you can see, I've the carbine to finish it here and now, if you've the mind,' replied Brad.

At that, there was the merest flicker of recognition in the second gunman's eyes and he smiled as he spoke.

'Easy there, friend. Ain't no need for gun-play; the lady might get hit. We're just errand boys delivering a message. So now that's done, we will be on our way. But Mr Hawker will expect a reply. No offence intended, Miss Jane.'

So saying, he doffed his white Stetson and then mounted his palomino horse which had an unusual white flash its right flank. This mark was well known to most law officers of Texas. So, as an occasional deputy, Brad should have recognized it, but he did not. As the owner of the strangely marked horse rode away, he turned and smiled. However, the gunslinger dressed in black was not so friendly.

'Like you say, stranger,' he said to Brad, 'you have the Winchester. Enjoy your advantage. But you won't catch me out again. Better leave today, because if we meet again, I'll kill you.'

Jane paled at the venom the gunslinger put into his words. But before she could speak, he too mounted his horse and then rode furiously after his fellow gunman. Jane turned to Brad.

'I thank you for your help, Brad, but that was Chad Dorrell. I'm afraid you've made a bad enemy there. He has a mean and ugly temper and a fast draw to back it up. They say he's outdrawn at least six men. So I guess you might want to take his advice and ride out after breakfast.'

'Ma'am, I'm not going to let words of any flashily dressed gunslinger worry me. But something about his friend does bother me. I think he might prove to be a far more dangerous man to cross. I don't suppose you know anything about him?'

She didn't. All she knew was that he had arrived in the area a few days ago and it had been rumoured he had been hired by the Blackwash Mining Corporation. Since he was riding with Dorrell who was one of the mine's top gunmen, it seemed that the rumour might be true.

However, according to Jane, the Blackwash silver mine had another, even more notorious gunman on its payroll. Yet he wore a badge. It was common knowledge that there was a lot of rivalry between them since they both claimed to be the fastest gunman in New Mexico.

So why would Hawker need a third fast gun? Apart from the expense, surely that would only add to the already existing rivalry? Brad pondered the puzzle, but not for long. The pangs of hunger turned his thoughts to breakfast.

A woman-cooked breakfast was a rare treat for a man who had lived on the trail since leaving Texas, so it was not surprising that Brad enjoyed every mouthful. However, there was something he had to get sorted out. Although there was plenty of money stashed away in his saddle-bags, he felt any offer of payment would be taken as an insult by his hostess. Instead, using his horse's lameness as an excuse, he made an offer he hoped Jane would find difficult to refuse.

'Ma'am, as it's going to be a few days before my horse is fit to ride, if you want, I could earn my keep working around your ranch until he's recovered.'

'Please don't keep calling me ma'am,' replied Jane. 'I guess if you're in no hurry to leave, the wagon needs fixing; the corral has to be rebuilt and the barn door needs mending. Then, if you don't mind doing even more mundane work, the house and barn could use a coat of paint. But I'm afraid I couldn't afford to pay you much.'

'Money's not necessary. A few breakfasts like the one I've just eaten and a bite to eat in the evening will be payment enough. I'll stay at least until my horse is fit to ride again. First, I'll fix the barn door so I can bed down in there tonight.'

'That will be fine,' replied Jane. 'It should be safe for you to stay at least a week. The Blackwash Mining Corporation have asked me three times to sell my ranch. Each time they have waited several days before returning for my answer.'

Brad didn't tell her he had no intention of leaving the Little U until he had discovered the whereabouts of Killner's gang. Besides, no true son of the Lone Star State would leave a woman alone in this wilderness, especially after she had been threatened.

But Jane had another problem.

'Before you decide to stay, I think I should tell you that Blackwash aren't the only ones who want my ranch. But the Little U is my home and is not for sale to anyone at any price.'

'That won't be the answer those gunmen or anybody else will want to hear.'

'No,' agreed Jane, 'but then it's not your fight.'

'Perhaps not,' agreed Brad, but in spite of his

overwhelming desire to track down Killner and his gang, something told him that it had a good chance of becoming so.

CHAPTER FOUR

It was late afternoon and hot; all traces of the spring storm had gone. From his seat on the porch in front of Blackwater's jail, Marshal Len Ward commanded a view southward down Main Street. The buildings were nearly all saloons, the largest and oldest of which was the Lucky Strike.

The Overland Stage depot straddled the southern end of Main street. It consisted of a combined ticket office and waiting-room, at the back of which was a large warehouse. Facing these, on the opposite side of Main Street, were Overland's large stable and smithy.

Some way beyond the Overland's buildings was a tall post, which marked the beginning of Blackwash County and the southernmost end of the town of Blackwater. The post also denoted the official limit of Marshal Ward's jurisdiction.

It was normally time for the marshal to make his rounds. But not today. Instead, he continued sitting on his porch waiting for the delivery of a very special parcel. The weekly Overland stage-coach had already arrived but he did not want to draw attention to the parcel by collecting it himself.

Fortunately, it was mid-week, so there were no miners or cowboys in Blackwater to cause any trouble. Therefore, he was surprised to see Sheriff Dent of Blackwash County ride into Blackwater.

For all his swagger, Dent had no legal jurisdic-tion in Blackwater. He was just an appointee of the Blackwash mine. But not only did the mine do a great deal of business in Blackwater, their miners spent most of their pay in the town's saloons. So Blackwater's town council had come to an arrange-ment with the mine. No objection to Dent's appointment would be raised so long as he only operated within Blackwash County.

But there was a major flaw in the scheme. Dent's fast and deadly draw meant few opposed him. So he went where he wanted, because the few who had disputed his right so to do, were now perma-nent residents of Blackwater's ever growing Boot Hill.

For that reason, Marshal Ward had backed away from a show-down with Dent for he knew he was no match for the county sheriff. So, once again, he pretended to look the other way as Dent dismounted and entered the main store.

Another depot marked the north end of Main Street. This one belonged to the New Mexico Territories Stage & Freight Company. Locally known as the New-Mexican, it was little more than a local freight line serving the large encampment at the Blackwash silver mine. It also owned several prairie-schooners specially adapted to carry miners to and from Blackwater. However, the New-Mexican's prized possession was a heavily armoured coach which, when escorted by Hawker's gunmen, was used to ship the silver-ore back East. Like the mine, the New-Mexican was owned by Jed Hawker.

The afternoon peace was further disturbed by Jane Latham as she drove her old and battered wagon into town. It had seen much better days, so its brand new back wheel looked strangely out of place. Seated next to Jane was a stranger and beside the old wagon was a fine sorrel stallion with a chestnut-coloured mane. Oddly, whilst its forelegs were walking, its back legs seemed to be trotting. However, the sorrel was limping badly on its right foreleg. Despite this, Jane drove straight past the New-Mexican depot which, like the Overland Stage, boasted a blacksmith.

As the wagon rolled slowly past the jail, the stranger dismounted. The sorrel seemed unwilling to follow the wagon, so the stranger hitched it to the jailhouse rail and then approached the still seated sheriff.

'Afternoon, Marshal. I'm Brad Miller. Used to work on the Double M back in Texas. I'm just a cowhand on my way to Arizona but I got caught in the storm and was offered shelter at the Little U. As I'm going to be working there for a while, I thought I'd better introduce myself.'

'I'm obliged,' replied the marshal.

It was something of a tradition in the West that a new arrival in any town should introduce himself to its lawman, especially if that new arrival was a gunslinger. Marshal Ward noted that, in spite of his claim to be only a cowboy, the stranger's six-gun was slung low across his right hip in a way few real cowboys would do since it might impede roping a steer, or be accidentally fired whilst still in its holster.

Then, there was the matter of the stranger's fine horse. The sorrel was clearly several rungs in the price ladder above the feisty mustangs normally used by Texas cowboys. Moreover, the stallion's magnificent saddle must have cost well over a hundred dollars.

Then, last but not least, word of the stranger's run-in with Chad Dowell was all over Blackwater. Few ordinary cowboys would risk incurring the wrath of such a notorious gunslinger. Indeed there were many who claimed Dowell was even faster than Dent. So the sheriff guessed the stranger standing in front of him was one of the Double M's gunmen.

The Double M was one of the biggest and best known ranches in Texas. It was noted for sending two herds per year to the rail-head towns such as Abilene and more recently Dodge. It was also notorious for employing gunslingers to ensure their herds arrived safely. As a result, even in New Mexico, there were few lawmen west of the Pecos who had not heard of the Double M or its redoubtable owner, Abe Mitchell. Since the end of the Civil War, he had not only defied the carpetbaggers, but had made the Double M into one of the wealthiest ranches in Texas.

But the code of the West dictated that a man was entitled to keep his past a secret. Moreover, handbills for Wanted men issued in Texas carried little weight in Blackwater since New Mexico was a territory and not a federal state. So all that concerned Marshal Ward was that the stranger stayed within the little law he was able to enforce.

'That's a fine-looking stallion you have,' he said. 'But I've never seen a horse move like that.'

'It's called a fox-trot. All his line move like that. Originally, they were bred in the Ozark region of Missouri, hence their name, Missouri Fox-Trotters. If you're on the trail all day, they are just about the most comfortable horse you could ride.'

'But not when they are lame,' laughed the marshal.

'He's only thrown a shoe,' replied Brad, 'but I had to ride him a mite too long before I could find shelter from the storm.'

'Hell, that was no storm, just a little Blackwater dew,' replied the marshal. 'If you're aiming to stick around, you might just get to see what a storm is really like.'

'Ain't got much choice at the moment,' replied Brad pointing at his horse.

'We've got two blacksmiths in town, but the Overland Stage's man is the best in this part of New Mexico. I could send word to have him fix up your horse if you like.'

'Be obliged, Marshal.'

'Will!' Len called loudly.

Will Langer came scurrying out of the jail. Much to Brad's surprise Will, who didn't look much more than seventeen, was wearing a star. His clothes were more appropriate for a sodbuster than a deputy. Although he carried a shotgun, he wasn't totting a six-gun.

'Will, take Mr Miller's horse down to the Overland and tell Max I'd like it reshod as soon as possible.'

It was clear that young Will had a way with horses. Although he did nothing more than speak to the horse briefly, Prince eagerly followed him to the Overland smithy.

'Two blacksmiths and two stagecoach lines, that's a mite unusual isn't it?' asked Brad.

'Guess so, but their rivalry isn't the main problem round here. There's a large silver mine about two hours' ride from Blackwater. Their land begins about twenty miles south of the Cactus Hills and they form the southern boundary of the Little U. It's common knowledge the mine owner, Jed Hawker, wants to buy the Little U. But even if Miss Jane wants to sell, he won't get it without one hell of a fight.'

'Why's that?' asked Brad.

'Because the land to the north of the Little U belongs to the Barr Zero ranch. Old man Barr was killed about six months ago in what was supposed to be a riding accident. His daughter, Kayleigh, claims he was beaten up by a bunch of the mine's gunmen, then left to die. But she couldn't prove it. In any case, they found his body in the wastelands between the Cactus Hills and the mine. My juris-diction only covers Blackwater.'

'So who runs the Barr Zero, now?' asked Brad.

'Kayleigh.'

'Another woman ranch owner?'

'Yep. But never underestimate Kayleigh Barr. She ain't much more than a kid, but in spite of her looks, she's got a mean temper and she's every bit as tough as her pa used to be. She hates the Blackwash Silver Mine and ain't about to let it take over the Little U.'

'How could she stop the mine buying the Little U if my new boss wanted to sell?' asked Brad.

'The Barr Zero ain't just any old ranch. It's fifty times the size of the Little U and employs almost as many cowhands as the Double M.'

'So, the Little U is a buffer between them,' said Brad.

'Yep. As long as Miss Jane doesn't try to sell.'

'From what she says, I don't she think will,' replied Brad.

'Good. But that don't mean I ain't got trouble coming,' said the marshal pointing at Sheriff Dent as he came out of the store which Jane had just entered.

Dent mounted his horse and then road slowly past the jailhouse. He barely acknowledged Ward. It was clear to Brad that the sheriff from Blackwash

County was no friend of the town marshal of Blackwater.

'Dent treats his star as a licence to kill anyone who opposes Hawker, but he is only authorized to operate within the limits of the mining camp. However, that doesn't stop him. As he's much faster than me with a six-gun, he does as he pleases.'

'Is he that fast?' asked Brad.

'Yes, some say as fast as Dorrell.'

'Any idea what brings him to Blackwater?' asked Brad.

'I guess he's looking for miners who have gone absent from the silver mine,' replied the sheriff.

'How come?' asked Brad.

Marshal Ward paused for a second before answering. This stranger seemed to be asking a lot of questions. On the other hand, he was working on the Little U and was entitled to know what he was getting into.

'I have an arrangement with the owner of the Blackwash Mining Corporation, Jed Hawker. His miners only come into Blackwater on pay-days and that is usually the twenty-first of each month. The miners stay until they are broke, which mostly takes no more than a couple of days. Then, Hawker uses his New-Mexican wagons to take them back to the mine. But some hide out. There's free travel on the Overland stage to Tombstone for any miner prepared to work there.'

'What about the hands from the Barr Zero?' asked Brad.

'I have a similar arrangement with the ranch. As the ranch pays out on the first weekend of the month, the miners are long gone before the cowboys arrive in town.'

'Sounds as if you've had some trouble between them in the past,' said Brad.

'Yep. Sometimes more than I can handle,' admitted Len.

'Well, if you ever need any help, just say the word. It wouldn't be the first time I've been a temporary deputy,' said Brad.

'I hope I don't have to take up your offer, but if I get to know you better, I may not have any choice. Apart from the usual problems, there's too many strangers around for my liking.'

Brad's interest heightened. Could any of these strangers be part of Killner's gang? But for all he knew, the marshal might be in league with them, so he refrained from asking any questions on the subject.

'I guess I'm another stranger to add to your list,' he said instead.

'Maybe not,' replied the marshal. 'Jane Latham is mighty particular who she hires, so if she is prepared to take you on, that's recommendation enough for me. Besides, your run-in with Chad Dorrell is all over town and he's no friend of mine.'

'Nor mine,' said Brad.

'Says he told you get out of the territory and been bragging he will call you out, next time he sees you.'

'Sorry to hear that,' said Brad calmly, 'but I'm not going to leave until I'm good and ready.'

'Guessed that was going to be your decision,' said the marshal.

'Blackwater also seems to have more than its fair share of saloons,' said Brad, as he looked down Main Street.

'Five so far. The Lucky Strike was built years ago when the Spanish used Blackwater as a stopping post *en route* to California. The rest have sprung up since the silver mining started. But these days we get a good many folks passing through to Tombstone, so even when the miners and Barr Zero hands are working, most of them get pretty busy in the evening.'

Could any of the folks passing through have been the renegades? From his own experiences at the end of each cattle drive, Brad knew saloon girls could be a good source of local news. So they might be his best bet to find out whether Killner's

44

gang had been in Blackwater. But which saloon would the renegades have used?

'Which saloon would you recommend?' he asked.

'Clem Mullet at the Lucky Strike has the best beer and prettiest girls in town. But take care if you like to gamble because I believe their tables are rigged even though I haven't been able to prove it yet.'

'Thanks, Marshal, but gambling isn't one of my vices,' said Brad.

'Well in that case, as I said, they have the best-looking girls in town. Alice Albright looks after them, but she doesn't live in the saloon like most of the girls. She has her own little spread, just out of town. She's a good friend of mine, so if you want a more private place to meet any of her girls, I could arrange it for you.'

'After I've caught up on the backlog of work on the Little U, I'll take you up on that offer,' replied Brad.

Alice Albright might be the best person to question about the comings and goings in Blackwater. However, the sound of the old wagon rumbling across the street heralded Jane's return and ended the discussion. But it was barely half full of provisions. She was not slow in relating the cause.

'The store would only let me have what I had the

cash to pay for,' she said indignantly.

'So that's why Dent went into the store. Seems like Hawker is going to stop at nothing to get the Little U,' said Marshal Ward who never called his rival by his appointed title.

'Is there nothing you can do?' asked Brad.

'Well, it ain't a crime to refuse credit,' said Len, 'but I'll call in on the store and find out what Dent has been up to.'

But before he could do so, his young deputy returned from the Overland depot. In his hands was the special parcel the marshal had been waiting for. However, there was no sign of Prince.

Will explained that the blacksmith, Max Gillard, thought it best for the stallion to rest up for a few days before he reshod it. Until then, the blacksmith had offered to keep Prince in the Overland's stable.

After the marshal's glowing testimonial, Brad could hardly refuse the offer. So the arrangements were confirmed and Brad left Blackwater as he arrived, a passenger in Jane's old wagon.

Few words were spoken during the trip back to the Little U. Jane was still furious about the general store's refusal to give her credit; Brad had other things to think about. Although he had picked up some useful information in Blackwater, he was no nearer to locating Killner and his gang.

CHAPTER FIVE

The following day, as Brad was repairing the corral fence, several riders approached the Little U. However, they were not from the Blackwash silver mine and although their leader wore men's clothes and rode on the distinctive, Texas style, cowboy's saddle, it was clear, even from a distance, the rider was a woman.

As she halted her men in front of the ranch house, it was also evident she was a woman of outstanding beauty. However, Brad soon discovered her temper was as short as her black hair was long.

'Fetch Jane Latham,' she ordered. 'I'm here to do business, not chat to the hired help.'

'I only take orders from Miss Latham,' said Brad quietly.

'Do you know who I am?' she said angrily.

47

'No, but I have no objection to you telling me.'

'I'm Kayleigh Barr, owner of the Barr Zero ranch.'

'Am I supposed to be impressed?' asked Brad.

Infuriated by his reply, Kayleigh savagely spurred her horse. The startled beast reared up, directly in front of Brad, as she had intended. In the same instant, she lashed out at him with her whip. To control the rearing mare using only one hand was an amazing feat. However, it was what happened next which drew gasps of astonishment from the assembled riders.

It was over so quickly, none of the watching riders could describe exactly how it happened. Somehow, Brad managed to side-step the rearing horse and, at the same time, catch hold of the whip in mid-air as it snaked out towards him. Before any of the riders could react, the whip was in Brad's hand.

Jane had been busily baking and preparing the evening meal when she heard the riders approaching. That she was content to let Brad deal with them was an indication of how much she had grown to trust the Texan during the few days he had been working for her. However, when she heard the familiar voice of Kayleigh Barr, she quickly made her way outside.

'Good morning, Miss Barr, would you like to

dismount and come inside?' Jane asked, ignoring the commotion caused by Brad's actions.

'No. I've come to buy your little ranch, not to socialize. The Barr Zero's offer is twenty cents per acre for all your ranch, including the hill land, paid in cash.'

'It's a fair offer, Miss Barr, and better than that of Jed Hawker. Even so, my answer is the same: my home is not for sale.'

'You may be holding out for another offer from Hawker, but if you try to sell to the Blackwash mine, you won't live to spend it,' said one of the riders.

Apart from Kayleigh Barr there were five other horsemen, but that did not deter Brad as his hand hovered over his Peacemaker.

'The lady has said she is not selling, so I don't take kindly to your threats,' he said coldly.

'My, you're the sassy one,' said Kayleigh, seemingly not in the least put out by having her whip taken from her, 'but there's no need for violence. We are happy to have the Little U as a neighbour, so long as it's under your ownership, Miss Latham.'

'That's mighty nice of you,' said Jane sarcastically.

'But nothing happens in the town of Blackwater or Blackwash County without our permission,' continued Kayleigh, seemingly unaware of Jane's sarcasm. 'So, if you ever change your mind, you must sell to us or face the consequences.'

'Which are?' asked Jane, her voice icily calm.

'Seeing your ranch house burnt to the ground and your range absorbed into the Barr Zero. Don't doubt that we will do it before any deal you strike with Hawker could be completed. So be warned. Sell out to Hawker and we will ensure that the Little U will disappear without trace leaving you with nothing!'

After issuing her threat to Jane, Kayleigh Barr gave Brad a long, deliberate look. She appeared to be not entirely displeased with what she saw and smiled as she spoke to him.

'We are behind in completing our round-up. There's long term work with regular wages at the Barr Zero. If you're interested, look me up.'

However, before Brad could reply, she wheeled her horse around and galloped rapidly away. The other riders followed quickly after her.

'Must be nice to have such friendly neighbours,' said Brad, attempting to match Jane's earlier sarcasm.

'Of one thing you can be sure,' replied Jane, 'the Barr Zero will back up their threat. Their bite is much worse than their bark! But as I said before, it's not your fight.'

Brad did not reply but over dinner that evening,

he voiced the questions that had been bothering him since his arrival at the Little U.

'Is there anything special about your ranch which makes Hawker and the Barr Zero so determined to buy it?'

'Nothing as far as I know. My ranch is tiny compared with the Barr Zero. It has about four thousand acres of decent pasture. Beyond that, about three thousand acres of hilly scrubland which leads to what the old-timers call the Cactus Hills,' replied Jane.

'Cactus Hills? That's a strange name.'

'Yes,' agreed Jane. 'The ground up there covered by a special cactus which only grows in New Mexico. In springtime, its flowers give off a scent like a lemon. But the ground is worthless. The Yampai live the hills, but not in the caves. They believe the spirits of their ancestors dwell in caves in the hills and only their medicine man is permitted to enter the caves to seek advice from them.'

'The Barr Zero's offer is worth a lot of money,' said Brad.

'Yes. But this ranch was my father's dream, so it's not for sale at any price!'

'I guess I feel the same about the Double M,' said Brad.

'Did you work there long?' asked Jane, but the

question was not as innocent as it seemed.

'I grew up there,' replied Brad, a little too proudly.

'And yet you left it to come to New Mexico,' said Jane shrewdly.

'But one day, I intend to go back,' replied Brad hastily.

The conversation had taken an awkward twist. Brad realized he was in danger of revealing too much about himself and the real reason for staying on at the Little U. So he changed the subject.

'Of course, what the Yampai believe about the caves is nothing more than superstition, but has anything unusual happened lately in the Cactus Hills?'

'Yes, Brad. A few days before storm, two prospectors went into the hills and have disappeared without trace.'

'Strange. Could they have passed through the hills and then got lost on the other side?'

'Not likely. Beyond the Cactus Hills, the ground becomes an open, semi-desert. It continues like that right up to the mining camp. Except for paydays there are usually over a hundred miners in the camp which is guarded by regular patrols. I doubt the prospectors or anyone else could get past them without being seen,' replied Jane.

'Well, their disappearance makes two mysteries,' said Brad.

'What's the other one?' asked Jane.

'I can understand the Barr Zero wanting to stop the Blackwash Mining Corporation from getting a foothold on their boundary line, but why on earth should Hawker be interested in taking over the Little U?'

'I don't know,' confessed Jane.

Brad thought for a moment. Could Killner and his gang be hiding out in the Cactus Hills? Perhaps the prospectors had run into them,? If so, the renegades would have had no qualms about killing them. But then again, surely someone at the mining camp have heard the shooting. However, the outlaws might have only stayed for a few nights and then ridden on to Arizona. There was only one way to find out. However, he was not ready to tell Jane the real reason he wanted to search her hills.

'After Prince has recovered, and if you agree, perhaps I might take a look at your Cactus Hills? Maybe I can find a clue to the whereabouts of the prospectors or even turn up something which might explain the reason why so many different parties want to buy your ranch.'

'Well it couldn't do any harm to have a look round,' said Jane, who was unaware that Killner might be holed up in her hills. 'In fact, to save time, I think I'll come with you. I could take you straight to the caves and act as your interpreter if we run into any of the Yampai.'

There was no way Brad was going to risk taking Jane into the Cactus Hills, even if a small part of them did belong to her ranch. Yet to refuse her offer outright meant he would have to tell her about the San Pedro massacre. He thought she had enough worries without adding to them, so swiftly changed the subject.

'You understand the Yampai dialect?'

'Just enough to get by on,' said Jane modestly.

Jane was unusually quiet for the rest of that night. Was it because he had shown no intention of leaving before the return of Hawker's gunmen? Or perhaps, she had something else on her mind?

However, he was too tired to care. Fixing the heavy barn door and mending the corral fences had been hard work. Once he could have taken the work in his stride, but in recent years, he had become unused to manual labour. As a result, he was exhausted and so decided to turn in. The hay in the barn's loft made for a warm and comfortable bed and he immediately fell into a deep sleep.

Next day was uneventful. Jane and Brad painted the ranch house. It took them all day but it was worth it. Brad was surprised what a difference a coat of white paint made to the appearance of the small ranch house. But the painting chores were far from over and the following morning found them painting the barn.

However, their work was interrupted by Deputy Will Langer. In spite of the dangers of the open range, or perhaps because of them, Marshal Ward had insisted that the young deputy was unarmed, except for his shotgun. Even in this lawless part of New Mexico, the sheriff believed that nobody would draw on a man not carrying a six-gun. Unfortunately, events were to prove the marshal wrong.

The reason for Will's visit was the return of Brad's horse. Prince had been reshod and had fully recovered from his ordeal in the storm. Indeed, the beast was back to his cantankerous self. Nevertheless, the boy controlled him with ease, never having to raise his voice above a whisper.

Brad was impressed. Once the Killner gang had been dealt with, he resolved to take the boy back to Texas with him. Since the murder of Seth Madden, the Double M was in need of a good wrangler.

The young deputy stayed for a leisurely lunch. Brad was glad of the diversion. Manual labour had long made forgotten parts of him remind him of their existence by inflicting considerable amounts of pain.

After lunch, Will headed back for Blackwater. It was the last time anybody saw him alive, except of course for the person or persons who shot him.

Chad Dorrell's fussily dressed companion found the body of the young deputy. The gunslinger claimed to have come across the corpse near the Cactus Hills. The deputy had been shot in the back.

However, the gunslinger strenuously denied shooting young Will, and he had actually taken the deputy's body back to Blackwater. After a long and private discussion with Marshal Ward, the gunslinger left. Since the crime had been committed in Blackwash County there was little Blackwater's town marshal could do.

Nevertheless, the marshal was puzzled. The Cactus Hills were not on the trail between the Little U and Blackwater. In fact, they lay in almost the opposite direction. So why had the young deputy ridden there?

To try to find out, Marshal Ward rode out to the scene of the crime and briefly searched it. Although there were tracks of several horses leading away from the murder scene and into the Cactus Hills, he decided against following them. Instead, he rode on the Little U to inform Jane and Brad of the tragedy.

Brad took the news badly. Had he not left Prince in Blackwater and agreed to Will returning the horse to the Little U, the young deputy might have remained in the relative safety of the town.

As soon as the marshal left, Brad also rode to the scene of the murder. As he had almost expected, amongst the many horse tracks, he discovered one which had a familiar v-notch in it. That, together with the cold-bloodedness of the crime, told a grim story to Brad, one the Texan thought best to keep to himself for the time being.

CHAPTER SIX

It was mid-morning and blazing hot. The late spring sun beat down with an intensity it usually reserved for mid-summer. In fact, part of the range beyond the stream was already turning into a dust bowl. Yet it was home to Jane's many hens. She had already clipped all their wings to prevent them from flying away, so now they roamed freely. But, perversely, they preferred to lay their eggs on the far side of the stream, out of sight of the ranch house. In spite of the heat, Jane was busily collecting them to sell in Blackwater the following day.

As Brad was finishing painting the barn, a lone rider approached the Little U. Brad recognized the rider's horse instantly. It was the palomino with the strange white flash on its flank. Its rider was the gunslinger who had accompanied Chad Dorrell when he had tried to persuade Jane to sell her little ranch.

At the time, he had seemed more friendly than Dorrell. However, had he been biding his time, waiting for the right moment to pay back Brad for their confrontation? Or was he merely calling to see whether Jane had changed her mind about selling her little ranch?

Brad was not about to guess the answer, so hurried into the barn. Seconds later he reappeared carrying his Winchester, fully loaded, cocked and ready to fire. But, surprisingly, the rider reined in his horse while the palomino was still well out of six-gun range. Nevertheless, the range was easily within Brad's Winchester. Once again the Texan held the advantage.

'Be obliged if I could set down a spell,' the gunslinger asked politely.

'So long as you keep your gun hand where I can see it and remember I have the Winchester, you're welcome,' replied Brad curtly.

The unusual white flash on its flank again stirred a distant memory. But Brad could not quite bring it into focus since most of his attention was focused on the right-hand of the gunslinger as he rode the palomino across to the water-trough before dismounting.

'That's far enough,' said Brad, as he raised his

Winchester to his shoulder. 'You can say what you want to say from there.'

'Fair enough,' replied the gunslinger. 'Is the lady of the house about?'

'No, but I can tell you her answer is still the same. You can tell your boss she has no intention of selling.'

'I guessed as much. Dorrell is busy at the mine, cooking up some plan with Hawker, so I volunteered to come alone to get Miss Jane's answer. But that's not the real reason for my visit.'

'In that case, why are you here?' asked Brad curtly.

'For the same reason as you,' came the surprising reply.

'I doubt that,' said Brad, still pointing his Winchester at the gunslinger.

'Seth Madden was kin of mine and a long time ago, I used to ride with your pa,' the gunslinger said quietly.

Brad swore quietly under his breath as he remembered. Almost two years ago Brad had been a temporary deputy and the gunslinger's description and that of the unusual flash on the palomino's flank had been on a Wanted poster. There was no doubt, the man standing in front of him was one of the most notorious and deadly gunmen Texas had ever known.

'I guess that must make you, Ethan Madden,' replied Brad, still pointing his Winchester at the gunslinger. 'My pa often talked about you, but the last thing I heard was you had been shot-up during a bank raid and arrested.'

'That's what people were intended to hear,' said the gunslinger mysteriously.

But Brad was in no mood to add another mystery to the ones he already had.

'So why are you here?' he asked again, this time a little more sharply.

'I need your help,' came the surprising reply.

'Why should I help an outlaw?'

'The raid you spoke of was about eighteen months ago. I just happened to be in Somerville when the gang struck. Its sheriff and me were old friends, so I tried to help him. But I got shot for my pains. For saving the bank's money, Governor Coke offered me parole. Then, after I recovered, he arranged for me to become a Texas Ranger.'

'I heard that the Rangers were back in operation again, but it's the first time I've heard them called the Texas Rangers!'

The one time outlaw carefully pulled open his jacket. Pinned to his shirt was a large silver star enclosed in a silver ring which bore the inscription, Texas Ranger on it.

'Texas was added to the title of Rangers when

Governor Coke got funds from the state legislature to reinstate them. But only a few rangers wear a star and there are several different versions,' admitted the lawman.

Brad lowered his Winchester and smiled.

'Before they were disbanded, the rangers were always welcome at the Double M. But I seemed to be forgetting my manners. Care to get out of the sun and come in for coffee?'

'Sure would,' said Ethan and followed Brad into the ranch house. 'Frankly, nobody was more surprised than me when I was offered the pardon and the badge. But whilst Miss Jane is not here, I want to talk about the Killner gang. I take it you haven't told her you're after them.'

'Too right! I've only told her that I worked for the Double M and I'd appreciate you telling her the same.'

'If that's the way you want it, then that's fine by me. Me and your pa go way back, but I was the one who used to kick over the traces,' replied the ranger.

'So he said. But although I've only been here a short time, that's long enough to see that the Little U has more than enough troubles of its own. It seems that everyone round here wants to buy it and won't take no for an answer.'

'I'm guessing there must be something special

about this spread we don't yet know.'

'You said you needed my help,' interrupted Brad.

'Yes. I think there's a fair chance Killner's gang is based in the Cactus Hills.'

'I'd come to the same conclusion,' agreed Brad.

However, he kept the details of the v-shaped horse track to himself. Ethan Madden had arrived at the silver mine some days before Killner's gang. So how had he known where to look for them? Brad had seen no proof other than a tin star to back up the former outlaw's story. And Madden was quite fast enough to have outdrawn almost any lawman he encountered. If he had done so, he could have then taken the star from the dead man's body and that man could have been a ranger.

'Have you ridden into the Cactus Hills?' asked Ethan, interrupting Brad's train of thought.

'Not yet. But Jane said there was a system of caves in the centre of them. For what it's worth, I think there's something very strange going on in the Cactus Hills, but it may not be connected with Killner's gang.'

'If it's not, what are the outlaws doing there?'

'I've no idea. Nor why they left a trail across New Mexico an Easterner could follow!'

'There are a lot of things about this which don't add up. But you're right; the first thing we need to do is to find out if the gang are really using the caves in the Cactus Hills for their hideout. Until I've checked that out, I don't think we should mention our chat to Miss Jane. But, for what its worth, I don't think it's in her best interest to sell the Little U—'

'Why would one of Hawker's hired gun-hands not want me to sell out to the Blackwash Mining Corporation and what's all this about a gang of gunmen on my ranch?' asked Jane from the door-way.

Brad had been listening so intently to Ethan he had failed to hear her return.

'Firstly, ma'am, I'm not one of Hawker's men, though I don't blame you for thinking so,' replied Ethan as he again displayed his star. 'I'm afraid it's probable that a gang of renegades has recently established a hideout in your hills.'

'But you are not absolutely sure?' asked Jane.

'No. Back in Texas, when I was working under-cover, I discovered the gang had a new hideout somewhere near Blackwater. The mining camp seemed a likely place, so I've been there with Chad Dorrell in the hope they might contact him, but until the killing of the young deputy, I hadn't found any trace of them.

'But, even if they had contacted Dorrell, why would he tell you?' asked Jane.

'I used to be an outlaw and for a short time rode with Killner. So, if Killner had a hideout in New Mexico, what could be more natural for me than to want to join them there?'

'You figure Dorrell is connected to the renegades?' asked Brad.

'Yes,' replied the ranger. 'If they are hiding out in the Cactus Hills, somebody in the mining camp must be supplying them with food. But whether Dorrell is secretly part of their gang, or they are all on Hawker's payroll, is anybody's guess.'

Jane was not convinced and voiced her doubts.

'Either way, what can you do? Surely a Texas Ranger has no jurisdiction in New Mexico?'

'Quite right, ma'am. But I intend to use my six-gun to persuade them to return to Texas and stand trial. But first I have to locate them. Then, I was hoping to borrow your man to help me take them back to Texas.'

'He's not my man,' Jane retorted rather too abruptly. 'In any case, you will also need a guide to get you round the hills. Someone who knows the back-trails and location of the caves. Otherwise you might blunder into them and find yourself outnumbered.'

'Do you have anybody in mind?' asked Brad.

'Me. It's still my land, so I'm coming with you,' said Jane.

'No, ma'am, it's far too dangerous,' said the ranger.

'If you knew just some of the terrible things these renegades have done, you would know the ranger was right,' said Brad bitterly, thinking about the San Pedro massacre.

'Nevertheless, I'm coming with you,' she said very firmly.

Brad's words made Jane look at him sharply. The suspicion that Brad had not been entirely open with her began to grow in her mind. Certainly, he seemed to know a lot more about the gang than he was letting on. Of course, it might have been a coincidence, but it seemed that if Killner and his men really were in the Cactus Hills, then Brad might be following them. If so, he was probably a bounty hunter and not the cowboy he claimed to be.

She found the possibility that Brad might have deceived her oddly upsetting. For some reason, the notion made her even more determined to ride with them. She had never met a bounty hunter, but some of the newspapers her father used to buy when they lived in New England regularly featured their activities and gloried in their often brutal killings. Yet somehow, she could not imagine Brad as a brutal manhunter.

Brad tried a different approach.

'Even if we agreed, you can't ride that great cart-horse,' he said.

'Then I'll borrow a pony from a friend who lives in Blackwater,' she retorted.

Brad tried again.

'Even if the Killner gang are in your hills, they won't be easy to find. So we might have to stay overnight.'

'And that means sleeping rough,' added the ranger.

'In that case we will need a pack mule to carry provisions and blankets,' she replied.

Brad's elder sister had been just as stubborn as Jane, so knew he was beaten. He glanced ruefully at the ranger who reluctantly nodded his agreement.

CHAPTER SEVEN

Two days later, the trio set out, but not until Jane had cooked a huge breakfast. Jane was mounted on a docile pinto pony which she had borrowed from her friend, Alice Albright. While she had been making the arrangements with Alice, Brad had bought a pack mule from Matt Gillard, the blacksmith at the Overland Stage depot.

It would have been a relatively short trip to the Cactus Hills had the trio ridden directly to them. But the relatively flat ranges of the Little U offered little cover, so they would been easily detected by any lookouts posted by the renegades. Guided by Jane, the trio rode parallel to the hills until they reach the end of them. Then she turned south and continued until they reached the arid scrubland on the other side of the Cactus Hills.

These scrublands, known as the wastelands,

stretched for miles and separated the Cactus Hills from the area owned by the Blackwash Mining Corporation. Although he had no legal title, Hawker regarded the area as part of his domain. So, several times per day, he sent out bugle blowing, cavalry-like patrols to back up his claim.

However, Jane had chosen this route because the wastelands was the home of a forest of giant cacti. Although tall cacti were not uncommon in the Texas Panhandle, Brad had seen nothing as remotely as big as these. Each one of them was as tall as a fully gown tree and many grew close together, forming perfect cover for any horseman.

As a result, the trio and pack mule were able to approach the hills safe from detection from either Hawker's patrols or Killner's band of oulaws. In spite of her companion's original doubts, Jane had begun to prove her worth as a guide.

The wastelands contained dozens of trails which criss-crossed each other as they circled individual hills or plunged into deep-sided ravines many of which were nothing more than blind or box-canyons which Jane expertly avoided. However, as dusk approached, she led them into a massive box-canyon, which also appeared to come to a dead end. But this one hid a secret known only to her and the Yampai Indians.

At first, it looked like any other canyon. However,

long ago, there had been an avalanche which had deposited a huge pile of rocks in front of the sheer cliff face. Jane led them beyond these rocks and continued right up to the canyon's towering cliff face. Only then did Brad see that there was a narrow track, far too narrow to be called a trail, between the rock pile and the cliff face. Although it appeared to lead to another dead end, Jane led them into it. They had to ride in single file because the track was so narrow.

In the gathering gloom, the unevenness of the ground caused Brad to rein in Prince and reduce his speed to barely walking pace. The ranger, following behind Brad and struggling to control the pack mule, was obliged to do the same.

No so Jane. In spite of riding side-saddle, she continued to ride her pinto at a steady trot. Consequently, by the time she reached the end of the passageway, she was a fair distance in front of the men. Then, to Brad's amazement, she and the pinto turned sideways and disappeared into the cliff face.

Risking all, Brad spurred Prince into a gallop. Unable to see what had happened, Ethan was taken by surprise and was left behind. In any case, the pack mule was proving to be less than enthusiastic about travelling along the narrow track and the ranger had to drag the stubborn beast behind him. He turned to rebuke the mule. When he turned to face forward again, Brad had also disappeared.

Yet the answer was simple. About twenty paces before the end of the passageway, there was a narrow split, barely wide enough to ride through. But owing to the peculiar configuration of the cliff face, it was not possible to see the split until you reached it.

Although it was almost pitch black, Ethan urged his reluctant palomino into the split and, leading the even more reluctant pack mule, gingerly edged forward. It took only a few minutes before he emerged into the gloomy light of an oval-shaped arena, but it seemed a lot longer.

The arena was totally enclosed by towering cliffs which contained several caves. By the time the ranger had emerged with the reluctant pack mule still safely in tow, Jane and Brad had already dismounted in front of one of them.

'Damn near got my head bashed in following you and Jane,' grumbled the ranger as he rode over to them.

'Sorry,' apologized Brad, 'but I didn't know what had happened to Jane.'

'Chancing after a pretty woman is likely to get you into a lot of trouble,' chuckled Ethan as he dismounted.

71

'Damn right! And I guess they don't come much prettier than Jane,' replied Brad, whose tongue had suddenly taken control of his mind. So the compliment was out before he could suppress it.

Jane said nothing but could not prevent herself from blushing deeply. But the men didn't notice. Evening approached and the sunlight barely reached halfway down one of the cliff sides and the floor was plunged into eerie darkness.

'Unsaddle the horses, while I check things out,' Jane ordered, as she tried to compose herself. Then she disappeared into the inky darkness of the cave before either man could object.

Without a word, they carried out Jane's order and also unloaded the mule. Then they turned the beasts loose to graze on tufts of wiry grass which were dotted about. The only way out was the way by which they had entered and neither horses nor mule would voluntarily enter that dark tunnel.

They had barely finished their chores when the pitch-black interior of the cave was suddenly lit up, revealing that it was nothing more than another small tunnel, even narrower than the one they had just ridden through. In the centre of it stood Jane, carrying an oil lamp. Without a word, she turned round and started to walk back down the tunncl. Brad followed with Ethan again bringing up the rear.

The floor fell steeply before leading into a surprisingly large cavern. An ice-cold breeze blowing in Brad's face made him shiver, but it suggested there might be another way out of the cavern.

The dim light of the oil lamp also revealed an enormous pile of tinder-dry wood, enough to last several weeks. There was also a large stack of cans of beans, several bags of flour, sugar and coffee beans. There were also two boxes of ammunition. Brad examined one of them and found that the ammunition matched that of his Winchester. Was this the outlaws' hideout? Jane swiftly dashed that idea.

'This cavern was used by the wife of the Yampai chief when she gave birth. But as she and her baby almost died, their medicine man said it contained evil spirits and forbad the Yampai to use it again. When Papa knew he was going to buy the Little U, he brought me here. It was his wish that the cavern should always be stocked with provisions in case the Little U was attacked by the Apache.'

'If nobody else knows of the cavern's existence, it would make an ideal base for us,' said Ethan.

'I'm glad you think so,' said Jane, smiling rather too smugly. 'As far as I know, apart from the Yampai and Papa, we are the only ones ever to set foot down here. So tell me, would you have found it without me?'

'It doesn't seem likely,' Ethan was forced to admit.

'Well, wait until tomorrow, you haven't see anything yet,' retorted Jane.

Knowing when he was well and truly beaten, Ethan retreated back up the tunnel and began to bring in the fresh food carried by the mule. Brad busied himself making a fire. The wood was so dry it blazed fiercely without emitting any smoke and the cavern soon began to loose its chill. Jane made a stew and they built up the fire for the night.

Unused to cave dwelling, Brad slept fitfully, twice rising to build up the fire. Yet, without the light of the rising sun to wake him, he slept through the unseen dawn. He was eventually roused by the smell and sound of bacon rashers sizzling and there were eggs from Jane's hens to go with them. Although he worried about the dangers they might yet encounter, even Brad had to admit that she had become indispensable.

But Jane had another surprise in store for them, but not until Ethan had watered the horses and pack mule. He did this by emptying his canteen into his hat and letting the animals drink from it.

As soon as he returned to the cavern, Jane picked up the oil lamp and led both men into yet another tunnel. This one was situated at the back

at the furthermost point from where they had first
entered.

After a sharp descent, they passed a small stream
which cascaded down a crevice, making it a simple
task to refill their canteens. Then the tunnel
levelled out and widened enough for the trio to
walk abreast. But as the tunnel began to rise
steeply, its roof became lower until they had to
crawl on their hands and knees.

Eventually, the tunnel burst out in the daylight.
Brad found himself on a high, craggy ledge shel-
tered by an outcrop of rocks easily large enough to
hide the presence of the trio. This ledge overlooked a deep, green and surprisingly fertile valley.
At the bottom of the valley, which sloped steeply in
a southerly direction, was a fast flowing river, still
swollen by the violent storm which had caught
Brad so unawares.

Along the river-bank was a large herd of cattle
engaged in prolonged bouts of drinking. In doing
so, they completely ignored the lush alfalfa all
around them. There was not a cactus to be seen in
this green and pleasant place.

'Jane, didn't you say the Cactus Hills were
completely barren ?' asked Brad.

'They are, apart from this valley. But the Yampai
told me that the river dries up by mid-summer.'

While Brad and Jane were talking, the ranger

extracted a pair of field-glasses from his saddle-bags, then studied the cattle very carefully.

'Miss Jane, is this valley on your range?' he asked.

'Yes. Officially the Little U boundary extends just beyond here.'

'I see. Care to have a look through my field-glasses?'

Jane took them and quickly scanned the herd. She instantly recognized the brand they were all carrying.

'All Barr Zero stock!' she exclaimed in amazement. 'But why would Kayleigh Barr put one of her herds on my land, especially as this part of it is quite near the Blackwash mine?'

'May I look?' asked Brad.

The frown on his face deepened as he carefully studied the herd through the field-glasses. Brad was an experienced cattleman and noticed the sides of the newly branded steers were bathed in sweat and lather. It suggested to Brad the herd had been spooked and stampeded last night.

'What do you make of it?' asked Ethan.

'That Kayleigh Barr and her men had nothing to do with driving the herd into your valley.'

'I don't understand,' replied Jane.

'Of course not, but if you had been brought up on a big ranch, like me, you might. Take another look through the glasses and tell me what you see.'

Jane did as she was bid, but shook her head as she saw nothing new, then returned the field-glasses to Ethan.

'But you can see the lather on their flanks,' said Brad patiently.

'Yes, of course.'

'So they must have been driven very hard or, more likely, deliberately stampeded. In either case, that's something the Barr Zero hands would have been desperate to avoid.'

'Why?' asked Jane.

'Because cattle are sold by weight on the hoof. Now on a trail drive, they will lose weight, so they are fattened up before starting on the drive. Then at least some of the excess fat should be converted into meat during the drive, thus reducing weight loss. Unfortunately, during a prolonged stampede, cattle will burn off a great deal of that fat and so lose more weight during the actual drive.'

'But couldn't the stampede have started acci-dentally?' asked Jane.

'Panic-stricken cattle may run wildly but they usually tire quite quickly and then it's much easier to turn the leaders and stop the rest of the herd.'

'But judging by their sweaty condition, they didn't tire quickly this time,' said the ranger.

'I guess they were repeatedly spooked to keep

them stampeding,' replied Brad.

'But who would do such a thing?' asked Jane.

'The outlaws, and I guess they ain't too far away,' said the ranger grimly.

CHAPTER EIGHT

Safely hidden by the outcrop of rocks, the trio kept watch from the ridge high above the valley floor. They had been watching for almost two hours, hoping that at least some of the rustlers would return. But none did. However, Jane thought she saw someone moving about in the rocks on the opposite side of the valley. But when Brad took over the field-glasses, all he could see were jack-rabbits and so concluded it was a false alarm.

He was wrong. But then as many a vexed trooper would verify, there are none better than the Apache at keeping out of sight.

Whilst they kept surveillance, a discussion about the rustlers took place. Brad thought they could only be Killner's gang, but the ranger expressed his doubts.

'Well, I guess it don't take much more than a few gunshots and a lot of yelling to spook a herd during the night, but what would Killner do with them?'

'You have a point. No rancher would buy Barr Zero stock unless the seller had a certified bill of sale,' agreed Brad.

'But don't rustlers usually rebrand the cattle they steal?' asked Jane.

'It's been known,' replied the ranger ruefully.

'Believe me, branding cattle is very hard work and takes a fair amount of experience, not to mention skill,' said Brad.

'I'm not proud of it, but as I said before, just before I left the outlaw trail, I rode with Killner's gang,' said the ranger. 'But I couldn't stomach the things they did. Even so, I got to know the regulars in the gang. None of them has handled cattle. In fact, they were the scum of the earth who would do anything for money except work for it.'

'So could the rustlers have come from the mining camp?' asked Brad.

'Although I remember meeting several Irishmen, most of Hawker's miners were Swedish, Dutch or Chinese immigrants. I don't recall meeting any former trail hands,' said Jane.

Brad looked taken aback at her revelation and

Jane realized she had nearly said too much. For some reason she could not yet understand, she found herself wanting to keep the details of her past life at the Lucky Strike Saloon away from him.

'Sometimes, I used to go to the mining camp with Papa,' she added hastily.

'Now you mention it, I didn't see any cowhands in the mining camp,' said the ranger.

Much to Jane's relief, the discussion was interrupted by the appearance of a rider, dressed entirely in black in the valley far below them and Brad didn't need the field-glasses to recognize him: it was Chad Dorrell.

The gunslinger dismounted by the river and allowed to his horse to drink. To those far above him, it seemed as if he was waiting for someone, since he showed no interest in the cattle all around him.

Ten minutes later, the suspicions of the watchers on the ridge were proved to be correct. Two more riders appeared, riding at a leisurely canter. However, even using the field-glasses, Brad did not recognize them, but the ranger did.

'The first rider is Nate Killner and the other is his number two, Reb Rosin. He's meaner than a rattler and twice as deadly. They call him Reb because he never stops boasting about the time he rode for Anderson's guerrillas and in his head, he is still fighting the Civil War.'

Brad felt nothing but hatred and revulsion as he saw the architects of the San Pedro massacre. Unaware of his presence, they made an easy target. But he had left his Winchester in the cavern, otherwise the two renegades would now be dead.

Unfortunately, the ridge was too far above the riders to hear their conversation, but it was quite clear that a heated debate was taking place between Killner and Dorrell. Rosin stood idly to one side, seemingly taking no part in the debate which lasted about twenty minutes. Then, all three mounted and rode up the valley. The ranger watched them closely through his field-glasses. It seemed that the two men were following Dorrell back to Blackwash mine.

The three on the ridge waited for another hour to see if any more outlaws came to tend the herd. None did. So, led by Jane, the trio made their way back down the tunnel and into the cavern. It was a surprisingly difficult descent. Brad found it much harder to crawl on all fours going downhill than he had crawling upwards. He was not the only one.

'One thing, for sure, I'm not cut out to be a miner,' grumbled the ranger as he clambered to his feet and entered the cavern.

Brad relit the fire and Jane cooked the rest of their provisions, leaving those already in the cavern largely untouched. Over the meal, they discussed what to do next. Jane was all for going straight to the Barr Zero ranch and telling Kayleigh Barr what they had just witnessed, but Brad disagreed.

'From what I've seen of Kayleigh Barr, that young lady acts first and thinks afterwards. She is quite capable of ordering her men to attack the mining camp. Even if we are right about Hawker, a lot of innocent miners could get killed.'

'Then I think I should go back to the mining camp,' said Ethan. 'If Killner and his side-kick are there, we will know for certain that Hawker is involved. If there's no sign of them, I'll poke around and find out if they, or any other strangers, have been seen.'

'Somebody ought to keep an eye on the herd in case Killner or any of his men return,' said Brad.

'Seeing they ain't real cattlemen, I doubt they will. Might be better if you both continued to look for their hideout,' the ranger suggested.

'Might be at that, but I can't risk taking Jane with me. You know what Killner's gang are capable of doing to a pretty girl.'

It was the second time Brad had indirectly paid

Jane a compliment and she again blushed with pleasure. The ranger noticed, but made no comment. Instead, he kept talking to Brad.

'Yes, you're right. Miss Jane had better stay here and keep an eye on the herd. As long as she is sensible, the rocks on the ridge should provide plenty of cover, so she's not likely to be seen from the river. I think she would be far safer here than in her own home with nobody to protect her.'

'Seems the best plan,' agreed Brad.

'When you two have quite finished talking about me as if I'm not here,' said Jane, having recovered her composure, 'I will tell you one thing: this is my land, so I will make the decisions. The first one being that I'm not skulking on the ridge, or hiding in the cavern, while you pair risk your lives!'

'But Jane, I'm just thinking of your safety,' protested Brad.

'You wouldn't have found the two members of this gang you seem to think is so terrible if I hadn't brought you here. And you still need my help to locate their hideout.'

'No, Jane, I won't risk your life,' said Brad firmly.

'Miss Jane has a point,' said Ethan. 'So, children, instead of arguing, why don't you both go back to the ranch house and collect the old wagon? You could fill it with supplies and bring it back here. If we do end up in here for any length of time, eating only beans and sourdough will soon get mighty tiresome.'

'We would have to go into Blackwater to get the supplies, but I doubt the general store would let me have them on credit.'

'No problem, I've got enough cash to pay for anything we need,' said Brad.

'So that's settled,' said Ethan. 'I don't want to alarm you, Miss Jane, but the Little U could be sitting in the middle of a range war. Common sense says we can't defend the ranch house by ourselves. But there's plenty of water in the cavern. As long as we got food and ammunition, we can hold it against a Yankee army, even if it was led by Grant himself.'

'Right then,' replied Brad. 'We can drive Jane's old wagon into Blackwater and I'll buy enough supplies and ammunition to last us a month.'

Jane looked in disbelief at Brad. Supplies in Blackwater were far from cheap. The silver strike and the influx of miners and new saloons had seen to that. Brad had already purchased the pack mule, which was for more expensive than an ordinary horse, so how could a dollar-a-day cowboy still have enough money left to buy supplies?

'Fine,' said Ethan, interrupting her train of thought. 'I would sure like to stick around until you two find out, but I've got to get back to the mining camp. I'll take the mule to explain why I've been away so long.'

'Find out what?' asked Jane.

'You will know *what* when the time is right, and my guess is that time ain't so far away,' he replied chuckling mysteriously.

'Ethan!' exclaimed Jane in exasperation. But he ignored her entreaties, picked up his saddle and, carrying it over his shoulder, walked awkwardly down the narrow tunnel towards the arena.

Jane looked questioningly at Brad, but he, too, had no idea what Ethan meant.

While Jane put out the fire and tidied up the cavern, Brad saddled up Prince and then commenced to saddle up Jane's pony. However, her European type of side-saddle had been designed to take a short stirrup. Not only did that make the task of controlling the horse more diffi-cult, it made tightening the saddle correctly absolutely essential. Yet Brad managed the tricky job with ease, unaware that Jane having completed her chores was watching him.

'It looks as if you've done this before. Does your wife ride side-saddle?' she asked, with much feigned indifference. For some reason, her heart was racing as she waited for his answer.

'I'm not married, but I've had years of practice with these side-saddles.'

'How come?' she said, desperately trying not to look too pleased about the first part of his answer.

'Pa is a bit old-fashioned in some ways. He insisted that all his girls rode side-saddle, even after the accident. Always said anything else was not lady-like.'

'Accident?' asked Jane.

'To my half-sister, Emma. She was some years older than me and always liked her ponies to be lively. One day, her favourite threw her as she was trying to jump across one of the streams on the Double M. Unfortunately, Emma was dead when the cowhands found her. They said the straps to her side-saddle had not been fastened correctly. I was only a boy when it happened, but from then on, I always made it my business to saddle-up my younger sisters' ponies.'

It was the first time Brad had talked about his family. Jane wanted to hear more, but there was work to be done. Reluctantly, she mounted her pinto, then led the way through the main tunnel and down to the passage way. As Brad deemed speed to be essential, she took the most direct route out of the Cactus Hills.

As they did so, the ranger reached the mining camp. He explained his prolonged absence by saying he had been trying to persuade Jane Latham to sell the Little U but she had again refused. Then, on his way back to the camp, he had found the pack mule. So he had decided to scout the cactus wastelands for its owner, but had found nobody.

Although Hawker was not convinced by Ethan's story, he had more important problems on his mind. Tomorrow was pay-day at the mine and seeing the miners got the right pay and then transporting them to Blackwater took a lot of organizing.

But that was the least of his problems. The mine was no longer as profitable as he had led its investors to believe. In fact, this month, there was only just enough money to pay the miners and next month promised to be even worse. The truth was, the mine was almost played out. Although New Mexico was only a Territory and law enforcement rudimentary, Hawker knew that the irate investors he had defrauded would find a way to ensure he faced several years in a penitentiary.

But Hawker had developed a ruthless plan which would rid him of the failing mine and make him one of the richest and most powerful men in New Mexico. After much preparation, all the players were now in place, so he decided it was time to make his first move. In spite of his doubts about Ethan Madden, tomorrow morning he would send him back to the Little U to run Jane Latham and her big-mouthed hand off the ranch. Dorrell could go with him to ensure Madden got the job done.

CHAPTER NINE

Brad and Jane reached the Little U just as night was falling. While Jane went to the kitchen to cook the evening meal, Brad led the horses and pack mule into the barn. They were greeted by a welcoming neigh from the cart-horse. Brad fed the great beast and ensured he had plenty of fresh water. Then he unsaddled and rubbed down Prince and Jane's pinto. He had just finished his chores when Jane called out that dinner was ready.

Not only had Jane cooked a superb meal, she had found the time to change into the one almost respectable dress she had kept from her saloon days. Nevertheless, its neckline was daringly low. Her hair was no longer tightly curled into a bun but hung loose and just touched her bare shoulders.

Brad was so astonished by the transformation,

he could hardly speak. However, much to Jane's amusement and pleasure, he eventually managed to splutter out a few incoherent compliments.

After the meal, there were several questions Jane wanted to ask Brad about his life at the Double M. Unfortunately, for her, he was extremely guarded about his private life and she learnt little that she did not already know. Soon afterwards, he retired to the barn where he fell into a deep sleep.

Not so Jane. Although she had the comfort of her own bed, thoughts of Brad kept her awake. She could not deny that she had begun to care for him. Why else would she have put on her best dress? But doubts about who he really was, plagued her mind. Whilst it was obvious he knew a great deal about cattle ranching, he had already spent far too much money to be an ordinary cowboy. Then, his words to the ranger came back to haunt her.

'*You know what Killner's gang are capable of doing to a pretty girl.*' Brad's words to Ethan suddenly came back to haunt her. She was pleased that Brad thought her pretty, but how did he know so much about the Killner gang? She refused to believe he was an outlaw. Yet, if he was a bounty hunter, why had he gone out of his way to help her? She eventually fell asleep still trying to work that out.

91

Early next morning, they set out for Blackwater. Jane drove the supply wagon; her pinto trotting passively behind it. The cart-horse was not made for speed but the empty wagon proved little challenge to the great beast, so they made relatively good time. As usual, Brad was mounted on his Missouri Fox-Trotter, Prince.

A little over an hour after they had left the Little U, Dorrell and Ethan arrived at the deserted ranch. Dorrell's highly inflated ego soon led him to believe Brad had left the territory rather than face him and that had finally persuaded Jane to quit the Little U. As Dorrell was eager to break the news to Hawker, they left immediately.

As soon as Jane and Brad reached Blackwater, they made for the store. However, still acting under instructions from Hawker, the storekeeper refused Jane credit. As he had promised, Brad paid in cash. The storekeeper reluctantly accepted Brad's money, but refused to help load the wagon. But help came from an unlikely source.

Acting on the instructions of Jed Hawker, Dent had ridden to Blackwater to prevent any trouble between his miners and any Barr Zero cowhands. Not that the sheriff expected any. Marshal Ward had so far managed to keep the miners and cowboys apart. However, Dent had another, far more profitable reason for riding into town.

But for the moment, his business would have to wait. Dent noticed the Little U's wagon outside the hardware store. Indeed, he could hardly miss the great cart-horse standing patiently before it. So he rode over to the store and decided to investigate.

'Morning, Miss Latham. Need any help toting your supplies to your wagon?' he asked, as he entered the store.

Jane was so taken aback by the offer, she could only nod her head in agreement. However, loading the wagon enabled Dent to check out the kind of provisions Jane and Brad had been buying. After examining them, the sheriff correctly guessed they were intended to provide meals on the trail rather than the relative comfort of the Little U's kitchen.

Of course, Dent was unaware of their true destination, so like Dorrell, concluded Jane had finally decided to leave her ranch. His suspicions seemed to be confirmed when, instead of turning the wagon round and driving back to the Little U, Jane drove out of Blackwater in the opposite direction and took the border trail to Arizona.

Hawker would want to be sure the pair were actually leaving the territory. Before he could follow them, Dent had some very private arrangements to make. However, his business shouldn't take long, so he anticipated no difficulty in catching up with the slowly moving wagon.

Because of the unwanted attentions of Marshal Ward, the Lucky Strike's gaming tables were set fairly while the Barr Zero hands were in town. As Hawker didn't want the Blackwash mine's straight-laced shareholders to know he owned the Lucky Strike saloon, he kept well away from it, so had no idea that the gaming tables were rigged when the miners paid their monthly visit to his saloon. The chief beneficiary from the ill-gotten gains was Dent, although the bartender, Clem Mullet, received a sizeable cut.

But Dent realized that the crooked tables could not go undetected for much longer. So while Hawker was still absorbed with his master plan, Dent decided the time was right to make one last financial kill and walked over to the Lucky Strike to make the arrangements.

Apart from a few saloon girls, the bar was almost deserted. Dent arranged with Mullet for the Lucky Strike's girls to serve as much free beer as it took to get most of the miners too drunk to notice that the tables had been rigged. Only then was the gambling started.

For those miners who were not drunk, Dent arranged another distraction. Those saloon girls prepared to put their charms up for sale were given leave to do so openly. As he had already bribed the mining-camp's pay-clerk to tell the miners of the treats in store for them at the Lucky Strike, they collected their pay and hurried to the covered wagons waiting to take them to Blackwater. If the clerks short changed them, they never knew.

By the time Dent concluded his business in the saloon, the first prairie schooner was almost due. So the bar had become full of saloon girls. Amongst them were some who had only just arrived in Blackwater and so not yet under the watchful eye of Alice Albright. Mullet offered the services of any of the new girls to Dent.

The sheriff of Blackwash Mining Corporation was eager to sample the delights of the prettiest new girl. As a result, it was some time before he hit the trail and headed after Jane's wagon. By that time, Jane had turned the wagon off the border trail. Brad had carefully erased the wagon tracks, so Dent missed their turning place and continued along the trail, unaware that the wagon was safely on its way to the hidden cavern in the Cactus Hills.

However, after a little while, Dent also turned off and headed towards the mining camp. Indeed, he actually rode along the edge of the wastelands and passed within a mile of Jane's wagon. But hidden among the giant cacti, even the wagon's dust trail was impossible to detect.

By the time the sheriff reached the mining camp, Dowell had already informed everyone still left there, that the Little U had been abandoned. Dent's somewhat abridged version of the day's events in Blackwater only confirmed Dorrell's story.

Jed Hawker was delighted with this news. But he was less impressed with the news that his latest acquisition had been questioning the miners about any new arrivals. But then, he believed that Ethan was an outlaw and a man on the run might reasonably be expected to ask such questions. So he let the matter rest and sent the undercover ranger on the evening patrol.

Hawker then dispatched Dorrell to Killner's hideout with instructions for the gang leader's next move. The time for action had arrived. Not content with taking over the Little U and thus provoking the Barr Zero into range war in which his own hired guns would make him the victor, Hawker then planned to take control of Blackwater. He intended to accomplish this by unleashing the renegades against the town. So now, maintaining the peace in Blackwater by keeping his miners and the Barr Zero cowhands apart was the last thing Hawker wanted.

'Time for you to deal with Marshal Ward,' he

said to the delighted Dent. 'Then, when things have settled down a bit, I'll see to it that you become the next marshal of Blackwater.'

CHAPTER TEN

The ranger had confirmed beyond doubt the link between Hawker and the outlaws. So as they rode into the wastelands, Ethan looked for a way to slip away from the patrol.

He planned to rejoin Brad and Miss Jane who, by now, should have returned to the hidden cavern. But with two riders behind him and two in front, even in the growing gloom of dusk, there was little opportunity to get away. Indeed, the unusual formation of the patrol suggested to Ethan that he was under suspicion. But that belief made him even more determined.

His chance to escape came in the most unexpected and alarming manner. Bugle-blowing patrols had ridden unchallenged through the wastelands since the departure of hostile Indians. But an arrow in the chest of one of the leading riders announced they were back. Suddenly, the patrol was beset on all sides as braves leapt out of the ground, seemingly from nowhere. Luckily for the ranger, apart from the dead leading rider, it was the two riders behind him who took the brunt of the attack.

In spite of the speed at which the patrol was galloping, the last two men were dragged bodily from their horses. At first, they put up a good fight. But they were soon overwhelmed. Tomahawks glinted in the dying rays of the sun and both men ceased to struggle.

As an arrow whizzed past his shoulder, Ethan savagely spurred his horse forward and the palomino responded instantly. The ranger desperately tried to follow the rider in front of him, but the man rode straight into a trap. More arrows sped through the air as another group of Indians suddenly appeared ahead of them.

The rider crashed to the ground, two arrows protruding from his chest. The palomino hurdled the fallen gunman who was still alive. But not for long. However, the Indians concentrated their attack on the downed man, enabling Ethan to gallop away. Spurring the palomino to even greater effort, he reached the safety of a large cluster of tree-high cacti and disappeared behind them.

Nevertheless, Ethan kept his horse at full gallop until it was almost exhausted. Only then did he stop and turned round. But the Indians had not followed him and that made him believe they were not on horseback.

The ranger had been too busy escaping to identify the Indians, but in this wild and desolate country, even on foot, almost any Apache could outrun a man on horseback. Therefore, the ranger reluctantly left his horse for the Indians but not his saddle.

He put on the moccasins he always carried in his saddle-bag then tied his boots together and strung them round his neck. Also strung round his neck was his water canteen. With his heavy Texas-style saddle perched precariously on one shoulder and his saddle-bag on the other, he toted a heavy load. The task was made harder as he also had to carry his Winchester.

Fortunately, there seemed to be little need to hurry. By the time the Apaches had dealt with Hawker's men and found his horse, it would be dark. Even if they had no alcohol with which to celebrate their victory, the ranger's experience told him the Indians would rest until dawn, by which time he intended to be near the hidden cavern.

The ground was so hard, Ethan guessed even

the most experienced Indian would find his trail hard to follow. In any case, he hoped any signs left by his Indian moccasins would confuse his trackers and throw them off the scent.

It was hard going, even for a ranger, and the heavy load slowed him down more than he expected. As a result, it was dawn before he reached the blind box-canyon. He paused to drink the last drop of the water in his canteen. Then he checked that he was not being followed. When he was sure that he wasn't, he ventured into the canyon.

His main worry now was the old supply wagon. It was far too big to be taken down the passageway or to be concealed at the blind end of the canyon. But he need not have worried: there was no trace of it to be seen.

But did that mean that something had gone wrong and Jane and Brad had not yet arrived? There was only one way to find out. So he proceeded down the narrow passageway as fast as his heavy and awkward load would permit. It seemed to take an age before he reached the schism in the cliff face. Then he turned into its inky darkness and inch by inch, groped his way into the arena.

Daylight had not quite reached the floor, although the top of its near vertical sides were bathed in the early morning sunlight. The cart-horse neighed its usual greeting. Jane's pony and Prince were too busy eating hay to acknowledge Ethan's arrival.

Thankfully, he dropped the heavy saddle and the saddle-bags. Then he made his way slowly down the cavern tunnel. Once again, he was immersed in almost total darkness. However, he had not gone far before he saw the flicker of light from the actual cavern. His voice echoed eerily as he called out.

'Hello, don't shoot; it's just your tired and hungry ranger paying a social call.'

'Well, come on in and help yourself to breakfast,' Jane replied. Strangely, there was much less echo when she responded.

'Where's the wagon?' Ethan asked as he sat down by the fire and helped himself to coffee and bacon.

'This is not the only hidden cavern in this canyon. It's riddled with passageways and secret caves. The wagon is hidden away in one of them. It's quite safe. You could ride right by the entrance, yet not see the wagon,' replied Jane.

Over breakfast, Ethan recounted his adventures. In spite of his narrow escape, he did not seem to be concerned. But Jane was shocked to hear about the attack by the Indians.

'In spite of what Hawker's men claimed, a war

party of Indians might explain why my Yampai Indians have disappeared,' said Jane.

'Possibly; except I think it was a scouting party of young bucks,' Ethan replied.

'What makes you say that?' asked Jane.

'They made a poor job of the ambush, otherwise I wouldn't be alive to tell the tale. Nor did they have horses or guns. In my experience, Apache war-parties usually carry plenty of both.'

'So you don't think they were Apaches?' asked Brad.

'Didn't get much chance to get on speaking terms with them, so I don't really know,' said Ethan, drily.

'Do you think the Indians are back for good?' asked Jane.

'No,' he replied. 'There's not much game here for them to hunt. My guess is that they are just passing through. But even if they are young and inexperienced, they are still dangerous. So I suggest we sit tight for a couple of days.'

Brad looked hard at Jane as he remembered the stories his father had told him about women captured by the Apache. Those who survived the ordeal gradually became so used to the ways of the Indian, they gladly become squaws and were absorbed into the tribe as full Indians.

'Agreed,' he said fervently.

'In any case, I'm too tired to move another inch,' said Ethan. 'If you two don't mind, I'll get some shut-eye.'

'Of course not,' replied Jane. 'While you are resting, Brad and I will go up to the ridge and keep an eye on the herd.'

'Good idea,' he replied. 'But don't expect any action. The Barr Zero hands are still out on the range finishing their round-up and while I was at the mining camp, Hawker sent a message to Killner.'

'Do you know what it was?' asked Brad.

'No, but I guess it was to lie low until Hawker is ready to make his move for the Little U. So I think it should be quiet for the next few days.'

For once the ranger was quite wrong. Even as he spoke, Dorrell was leading most of the mining-camp's gunmen across the wastelands. They were headed to the Little U. Then, while Dorrell and his men were safely out of the way taking possession of the ranch, Killner and his gang rode into the mining camp, guns blazing.

Not that there was any opposition. Before dawn, Hawker had driven away in the New-Mexican's special armoured coach which was laden with silver ingots he had secretly stashed away.

Dent had left the camp even earlier and was on his way back to Blackwater, supposedly to keep an eye on the miners. However, the real purpose of the trip was to check on how much money he had made from the rigged tables. But he also had some unfinished business with Marshal Ward to settle.

So the encampment at the Blackwash mine was almost deserted. There were just the pay clerk and a handful of miners. The latter preferred to send their hard-earned pay back to their families, rather than gamble it away in the Lucky Strike saloon.

Guns roaring, the renegades rode into the mining camp, killing anyone in sight. However, Killner was careful to leave a couple of miners alive to bear witness to the damage caused by the rampaging outlaws. Of course, the survivors would have no idea that the gang's carefully orchestrated raid was part of Jed Hawker's master plan, but they would be able to recount the horrific events to the rest of the miners when they returned from Blackwater.

Unfortunately, the camp's clerks were not as lucky as the two miners spared by Killner. They worked, not in the camp, but in two cabins near the mine entrance. Their function was to deal with the mine's accounts. They also recorded all the mine's day-to-day transactions, especially the amount of silver mined and how much had been shipped back East. So they had to be eliminated, a task the gang performed without the slightest sign of mercy.

Next, they set fire to both the clerks' cabins and watched while they burned to the ground. Thus all the records of the mine were destroyed. However, their last act of wanton destruction concerned the mine itself. They set charges and dynamited the entrance and watched, gleefully, as it collapsed amidst a shower of rubble and plumes of blinding dust.

With the mine inoperable, Hawker believed that its miners would head for Tombstone, especially if the New-Mexican provided them with free transport. Thus in one stroke, he would be freed from the prying eyes of the mine's shareholders and, with no miners to guard, his gunmen would be free to fight the Barr Zero. Taking control of the Little U was simply to draw the hot-headed Kayleigh Barr into a range war which, with the help of Killner and his cohorts, Hawker felt sure he would win.

But destroying the mining camp was hungry work. For this reason the camp's cook had not been harmed. With the aid of the two miners they had spared, the cook was forced to prepare them a meal which they ate with relish. Then they showed their gratitude by burning the cookhouse to the ground.

106

However, far from being satisfied with the mayhem and destruction they had wreaked at the mine, the renegades mounted their horses and rode towards Blackwater. But they were in no hurry. They laughed and joked as they made their way slowly towards the border trail and on to Blackwater, knowing their day of wanton destruction and wilful murder was only just beginning.

CHAPTER ELEVEN

Dent arrived in Blackwater an hour after dawn. As he expected, except for the small but always busy office of the New Mexico Territories Stage & Freight Company, the town was almost deserted. He swaggered into their office and then ordered the clerk to ensure its prairie schooners were made ready and sent round to the Lucky Strike within the hour.

The New-Mexican was, of course, part of Hawker's growing empire, so the clerk scuttled away to get things organized. Drivers had to be awakened and the stable boys had to tend to the horses before they could be harnessed.

Usually, the miners were allowed to stay in Blackwater until they had spent all their hard-earned pay in the Lucky Strike saloon. But not this time. Hawker had told Dent to get them back to the mining camp to see the havoc inflicted on the camp.

Having ensured that the orders of his boss were carried out, Dent made his way to the Lucky Strike. The town was still deserted, but, as he entered the saloon, he discovered that Clem was restocking the bar and not in his private office counting their ill-gotten gains. The reason was clear. The saloon had an unwelcome visitor. Acting from a tip-off from his friend Alice Albright, Marshal Ward was busily examining the gaming tables.

'Clem, what's he doing in here?' asked Dent.

'Said he's had a complaint from some of your miners that the tables were rigged. He's been nosing around in here for the last halfhour, checking things out. But don't worry, I've already reset the tables. He won't find anything.'

But Clem Mullet was wrong. He had been too greedy. Not content with the cut from the rigged tables, without Dent's knowledge the bartender had instructed his dealers to use loaded dice. Unfortunately for him, the floor of the saloon had not yet been swept.

Marshal Ward suddenly stopped examining the tables and stooped down. He retrieved two small objects off the floor. An experienced gambler in his younger days, it only took the marshal a few seconds to determine the die were loaded.

Completely ignoring Dent, Blackwater's law offi-cer approached the Lucky Strike's bartender.

'Clem Mullet, these die are loaded. I'm arrest-ing you for running a crooked gambling house.'

'You're arresting no one,' snarled the sheriff of the Blackwash mining camp.

'Dent, what you do in your mining camp is none of my business, but here in Blackwater, I'm the elected marshal. So I suggest you complete any business you still have to do, sooner rather than later. But finished or not, I want you out of town by noon.'

'What makes you think you're man enough to make me go?' sneered Dent, remembering how many times the man in front of him had deliber-ately avoided a showdown.

Marshal Ward didn't answer the question. Instead, his eyes glanced at the bartender who was stealthily inching his way towards the end of the bar.

'Stay where you are, Clem!' he ordered. 'Better you leave that special shotgun you have hidden under the bar where it is. The next move you make towards it will be your last one!'

'That's big talking, Marshal Ward,' said Dent coldly. 'Think you can back it up with me here?'

Blackwater's law-enforcement officer looked

straight at his nemesis and then, very deliberately, stepped to within a few paces of him.

'Better not try to find out,' he said quietly.

But, of course, Dent had to. He couldn't back down without ruining his reputation as a top gunslinger. And Dent was supremely sure of himself, for he had already proved that he was faster than his opponent. So, full of confidence, he went for his six-gun.

The hammer blow to Dent's abdomen forced him to double up, causing the bullet from his own six-gun to hit the floor directly in front of him. Then he slumped to his knees clutching his stomach with his left hand in a vain attempt to staunch the blood pouring out of it.

His six-gun dropped from his other hand. His stomach seemed to be on fire and he felt real pain for the first time in his life. Yet the sheriff knew it could only get worse. None of the men he had deliberately gut-shot had lived to tell the tale. Most had survived a few days, suffering in terrible agony before they eventually died.

Determined not to suffer that fate and driven onwards by his pride, Dent stretched out a blood-soaked hand and retrieved his six-gun. Then, as Ward watched him, he slowly replaced it in his holster. Summoning the last of his rapidly failing strength, the sheriff clambered slowly to his feet.

The effort only served to intensify the pain in his stomach.

Dent looked at the marshal's six-gun. Then a glimmer of understanding penetrated his agony. The reason Ward had stood so close to him when he drew became clear, for the six-gun grasped firmly his hand had the shortest barrel he had ever seen.

'It came in on the last stage,' the marshal explained. 'It's Colt's latest offering. They call it, the *Sheriff's Model.* Rather an apt name in the circumstances. But in spite of its shortened barrel, it's still a Peacemaker .45.'

It soon became evident to the law officer that his adversary was no longer a threat and was in great pain. So he holstered the snub-nosed, Sheriff's Model Peacemaker and went to aid his stricken foe. But Dent was not yet done and seized the chance to draw his own six-gun again. It was his last error of judgement.

Again the four and three-quarter inch barrel of the snub-nosed Peacemaker spat its deadly message. This time the bullet struck the sheriff full in the chest. The force of the impact blew him off his feet and into oblivion, his conventional seven and a half-inch barrelled Peacemaker, only half-drawn.

Yet in death, there was a smile on Dent's lips. His

pride was still intact. He had not been outdrawn, just outsmarted by Ward's newfangled six-gun. And the agonizing pain in his stomach was no more.

Without so much as a glance at the prostrate body, Marshal Ward stepped over it and hand-cuffed the bewildered Clem Mullet. Once the bartender had been secured, Ward holstered his six-gun. Although the edge the gun gave him could only be short lived, he did not want to adver-tise his newly found advantage.

Although it was still early, drawn by the shoot-ing, a crowd of miners and saloon girls began to assemble in the bar. There were audible gasps of amazement when they saw the body of Dent lying in a pool of blood. The excited babble which broke out seconds later, almost drowned the sound of several prairie wagons drawing to a halt outside the Lucky Strike.

'Folks, the show's already over,' said Marshal Ward. 'Clem Mullet is under arrest for running rigged tables, so the Lucky Strike is temporarily closed.'

'We want our money back,' shouted several of the miners in unison.

'Naturally,' replied the marshal. 'But not today. It will have to be counted first. But don't worry, I will see to it that all last night's takings will be refunded by the town's committee as soon as possible.'

Some of the miners began to complain, but their compatriots soon told them to shut up. After all, before the gunfight, there had been no chance of getting their money back.

'Now,' continued the marshal, 'I'm pretty sure the wagons have just arrived to take you miners back to the mining camp. So, if you would make your way to them, I would sure appreciate it.'

Nobody was going to court the wrath of the man who had just outdrawn the sheriff of Blackwash County. So the miners trooped out to the prairie schooners and left Blackwater as quickly as possible. And it was just as well they did for a little over an hour later, Killner's gang came sweeping into Blackwater, guns blazing.

Their target was the bank. The new Sheriff's Model, so deadly at close range, was of little use against any target more than a dozen paces away, but that didn't stop Marshal Ward from trying, although it was more by luck than judgement that he hit one of the gang. But without any deputies to back him up, he was forced to take cover and could only watch helplessly as Killner's gang robbed the bank. But they had not finished: they set fire to it.

But, at first, it burned poorly. While the renegades were concentrating on getting the fire going, the marshal began to work his way back to his office. But it was slow progress. Two of the gang mounted their horses and rode up and down the main street shooting indiscriminately at anything that moved. So the marshal had to use every scrap of cover he could find. It seemed to take an age, but eventually he reached his office throwing himself through its half-open door as bullets whistled over his head.

Once inside, Ward paused only to regain his breath. Then he grabbed his Winchester. Disregarding the danger of flying bullets, he dashed back down the street towards the bank. However, satisfied the building was ablaze, the rest of the outlaws had already mounted and were ready to ride away.

Nevertheless, the marshal took aim and opened fire. One member of the Killner gang bit the dust, but the rest galloped safely away. However, their absence was to be short lived.

Huge flames towered over the blazing bank, posing a real threat to the neighbouring properties. Belatedly, some of the townsfolk left the safety of their homes and began to put out the fire. But they were too few and too badly organized to control the blaze. So, instead of raising a posse and chasing after the perpetrators, the marshal stayed in Blackwater and organized the fire-fighting.

However, the bank was a roaring inferno and too far gone to be saved. So the marshal organized the townsfolk two-abreast in two separate lines which ran from the town's only public water pump to each side of the blazing building. Pails of water ran along one side of each human chain and were poured, not on the blazing bank, but on the buildings either side of it. The empty pails were then returned down the other side of each human chain to be filled at the pump. In this way, the fire was prevented from spreading, but the bank was burnt to the ground and all its records lost.

The loss of the bank's records and those held in the clerks' cabin at the mine were the real reasons why Hawker had so carefully organized this day of destruction. Without records of any sort, the shareholders, the real owners of the Blackwash Mining Corporation, would have to believe any story he chose to tell them.

But Hawker had underestimated Killner. New Mexico was a Territory and officially, not yet part of the United States. Although the US Cavalry carried out patrols, they were mainly concerned with Indians, who, unlike many of their Texas cousins, still remained a major and deadly threat. So there would be little federal law to bother them in New Mexico.

116

With the miners gone, Killner realized the isolated town of Blackwater would make a perfect base for the gang's operations. Once they gained control of the town, the renegade leader believed they would meet little opposition. With the money from the bank in his pocket, Killner could offer Hawker's gunmen top pay. Also, with the town under his control, he could also provide them with the delights readily offered by the saloon girls and that must be better than guarding an empty mining camp or patrolling in the harsh environment of the wastelands.

After checking there was no pursuit, Killner brought his riders to a halt and outlined his plans. They would return to the caves, but only for the night. Tomorrow, they would return to Blackwater and kill anyone, including Hawker, who opposed them.

CHAPTER TWELVE

It was almost noon. High on the ridge overlooking the rustled Barr Zero herd, Jane at last plucked up courage to question Brad about his past life. Even so, she couldn't bring herself to ask him if he was a bounty hunter.

'If you are just a cowboy, how come you know so much about the Killner gang?' she asked instead.

If Brad was surprised by her directness, he did not show it. Instead, he smiled. 'It's a long story,' he said.

'So what! I guess we will be here for some time,' she said pointedly.

Brad nodded in agreement. Perhaps it was time to tell Jane the truth, even if it was not quite all of it.

'I grew up on the Double M. As soon as I was old enough, I became a wrangler. I was barely sixteen when I made my first cattle drive. It was the year after the end of Civil War. The Double M was heavily in debt and virtually bankrupt. Then, using the carpetbaggers law, the Yankees tried to take the ranch from us. But the ranch still had a few influential friends and they bought us enough time to take five hundred steers up the old Shawnee trail to Kansas City. We barely made it.'

'Did you run into Indians?' asked Jane. She had become so enthralled by Brad's reminiscences, she had quite forgotten the original purpose of her questions.

'Only tame ones who wanted a steer or two for crossing their lands. No, it was the Kansas farmers and their cronies who caused the trouble. They had all but closed the trail. Unfortunately, there was some shooting before we got the herd into Kansas City. Then they caught up with us and demanded more compensation and we had to pay a quarter of the money we got for the herd and give them all our mustangs before they dropped their charges against us.'

'So how did you get back to the Double M?' asked Jane.

'By train to New Orleans and then by ship to San Diego. I was seasick most of the time and have never been on a ship since!'

'But the mortgage was paid off?'

'Barely. There was not enough money left over to see us through to the next trail drive and the banks would not loan us any money. However, the neighbouring ranch had been bought by a wealthy English family but run by Texans and they a offered to add a hundred of our cattle to their trail drive. With that extra money, we survived until the following round-up. Then we took fourteen hundred cattle to Abilene, and the year after two thousand. In spite of the carpetbaggers, we continued to prosper and a few years later we began to make two drives a year.'

'That must have been very hard work.'

'Yes, but I was a lot younger then and enjoyed every minute. By the time I was twenty, I had made seven drives up the Chisholm trail to Abilene and was trail boss by the time I was twenty-two. Then we switched to the western trail and took our herds into Dodge. After another three of years I became the Double M's top hand. So I guess I've earned the right to be called a cowboy.'

'But that doesn't explain how you know so much about the gang of outlaws you say are on my little ranch.' protested Jane.

'A few months ago, Killner's gang raided San Pedro, a small Mexican settlement on the edge of the Double M's range. None of the Mexicans were armed. Because most of its people worked on the

Double M, the settlement was supposed to be under our protection. But that didn't stop Killner's gang from raiding it, butchering men, women and children in the process. Yet they deliberately left a few alive to tell to tell the tale.'

'But why did they do such a terrible thing?' asked Jane.

Brad was about to reply when two muffled gunshots echoed round the cavern far beneath them. He thrust the Winchester into her hands.

'Stay here. Shoot at anybody coming up the tunnel who's not singing.'

Without waiting to hear her objections, Brad drew his six-gun and began to make his way back down the tunnel. But again, he found the descent far harder to manage than the climb up to the ridge. More shots rang out, but as he didn't know who else might have discovered the cavern, he had to complete the first part of the descent in darkness. Fortunately as he neared the end of the tunnel, the flickering light of the camp began to light his way. He arrived in time to witness a desperate scene.

In spite of their youth and inexperience, the Indians had managed to track the ranger right into the cavern. For their troubles, two of them lay dead, but the Texas lawman was desperately grappling with two more. One of his six-guns, now empty, lay uselessly on the ground. Strangely, the other remained in his cavalry-style holster and the big Texan had resorted to using the Bowie knife he always carried. But its blade only sliced through open air as one of the remaining Apaches swayed back out of reach and then darted behind the blazing fire. The pan of bacon suspended above it prevented the ranger from striking at the Indian again.

The second Indian lunged forward, tomahawk raised aloft, ready to bury it into Ethan. But Brad's bullet struck its blade and smashed it into pieces before he could do so. Nevertheless, the Indian still managed to fling himself onto the Texas lawman. Brad could not risk shooting again for fear of hitting the ranger.

Engaged in a life-or-death struggle, the ranger could not also defend himself against the first Indian. So Brad flung his Colt aside and hurled himself into the fray. He tackled the one still crouching behind the fire. But his wily opponent soon got the upper hand and this Apache now had a knife.

It would have been all over for Brad had the cavern not been filled by the sound of a rifle shot. Its impact flung his would-be assailant across the cavern floor. Amazingly, he seemed to recover. With blood oozing from a chest wound and knife in hand, the Indian staggered towards Brad. But the echoes of the first shot were still reverberating against the cavern's walls as the second shot hit the Apache. This time, the brave died instantly.

The remaining Indian fared no better. The Texas lawman was an old Indian fighter, so was far too experienced for his much younger attacker who tried to ensnare the ranger in a head-lock. But Ethan swiftly fought himself free and then, almost faster than the eye could detect, his knife struck and the young Indian buck ceased struggling.

Brad turned to face his saviour. Standing in the mouth of the ridge tunnel was Jane. Even in the flickering firelight, her face was as white as a ghost. Fortunately for Brad, she had ignored his orders and followed him. The Winchester he had given her on the ridge, still nestled firmly against her shoulder.

Ethan picked himself up and then smiled ruefully.

'I'm getting too old for this game,' he said ruefully. 'I let these young bucks sneak up and nearly take me. I got two before my six-gun misfired and then jammed. The other two were on top of me before I could get to my other one, so I had to use my old Bowie knife.'

Brad stooped down and picked up the six-gun. Its hexagonal barrel gave away its age. But, surprisingly, the gun appeared dark yellow in the light of the camp-fire.

'It looks like a very old Colt. One of the early Navy models; but if it is, it's the first one I've seen with a brass frame,' he said, returning it to the ranger.

'It's been my companion for many years, but it's not a Colt. You were a mite young to serve in the Civil War, so you wouldn't have seen a gun like this. I guess it's one of the last still in use,' replied the ranger, still smiling ruefully.

'So what is it?' asked Brad.

'It was made in the South by Griswold and Gunnison. It's an exact copy of Colt's .44 Navy "Old Model". But they were made out of brass because the South had run short of metal.'

'Do you still have to make up your own ammunition?' asked Brad.

Ethan nodded his head in affirmation.

'Then it's definitely time you changed,' said Brad firmly. 'When this job is finished and your duties bring you near to the Double M, come and visit us. Although we don't allow our hands to carry guns around the bunkhouse, we have an arsenal in the house in case of an emergency.'

'I have a brand new gun in my saddle-bags. Cost me more than a month's wages, but it's no good for close range shooting. So I still need to replace the Griswold as soon as I can afford to do so,' replied the ranger, smiling broadly.

What kind of six-gun was no good at close range, wondered Brad? Then he remembered that the ranger's basic pay was only one quarter a day more than his dollar-a-day cowboys, and a mail order Peacemaker cost seventeen dollars. A splendid idea came into his head. Ethan might help him solve a tricky problem which might arise on his return journey to Texas. But as that problem involved Jane, he didn't mention it directly.

'I've got a better idea,' he said instead. 'After we've finished here, travel back to the Double M with me and I'm sure we can sort out one of the latest Peacemakers for you. Or you could have a new Remington, if they are more to your taste.'

'Fine,' agreed the ranger. 'I'd like to pay my respects at my cousin's grave. But I guess I'd be a goner without your help and I haven't thanked you. But you were a damn fool to charge into the fight, unarmed.'

The danger over, Jane began to shake all over. Brad took the rifle from her and was too busy comforting her to acknowledge the ranger's gratitude. So Ethan turned his attention to the dead Indians and began to examine them.

'Well I'll be damned!' he exclaimed. 'They are Apaches, bar one. But their markings show they are from a sub-tribe I recollect hearing about when I was a boy. But the one you killed, Miss Jane, ain't even an Indian!'

'What do you mean?' she asked.

'He's white.'

'Oh no! What have 1 done?' gasped Jane in alarm, reluctantly disentangling herself from the comfort of Brad's arms.

'Saved your man's life,' replied the ranger, 'but we can talk later. We had better get out of here, pronto. We can defend ourselves against a Yankee army but Apaches, that's different. By now, the rest have probably stolen our horses and there's no telling how many more of these red devils are on their way here.'

By the light of the last remaining lantern, they cautiously made their way out of the cavern into the arena. But there was no need for concern for all three horses were busily grazing on the little grass that still remained. There were no signs of other Indians.

Although there were literally countless numbers of wild mustangs roaming in the Texas panhandle and in the wilds of New Mexico, stealing horses was a way of life for the Apache. Braves who did so gained almost as much prestige and honour as killing the hated white man.

Oddly, although it was self evident that some of

126

the Indians in the raiding party did not possess horses, they had chosen to fight rather than steal them. To the ranger, that suggested these nomadic Apaches were young bucks, probably the worse for liquor and spoiling for a fight.

Nor had the Apaches found the old wagon which still contained most of the food Brad had bought in Blackwater. As he hitched the cart-horse to it, Ethan stood guard. Then, while Brad scouted the trail ahead of them, Jane drove the wagon out of the hidden ravine. Ethan sat beside her, Winchester at the ready, but they saw no one.

Jane remembered their conversation just before the ranger had left for the mining camp. Indeed, his remarks had bothered her ever since and this was her chance to quiz him on the matter.

'Ethan, what did you mean when you said you wanted to be around when I found out? Found out about what?'

Instead of answering her directly, Ethan stared pointedly at Brad, just visible in the distance. So pointedly, Jane blushed profusely.

'I thought so,' he said, and his weather-beaten face broke out into a huge grin, 'but the fun won't start until our boy finds out too!'

'I don't know what you mean,' replied Jane still blushing.

'I think you do, and he's quite a catch, by the way.'

127

'I still don't know what you mean,' protested Jane.

'What do you think the Double M stands for?'

'I guess it's something to do with its owner,' replied Jane.

'Partly. The ranch was founded by Luke Mitchell just after Texas won its independence from Mexico. He called it the Crazy M. At first, it was just a small collection of shacks deep in the Panhandle. They weren't even proper ranchers, just a few men who rode to the Brazos River, rounded up a hundred or so wild longhorns and drove them up the Shawnee trail to the railhead at St Louis. My pa was one of the drovers but got himself killed by Indians on the third drive.'

He paused. Although it was many years ago, the hurt still remained. 'Go on,' said Jane gently, sensing he had not talked about his past for a long time.

'When I was young I rode a wild trail. Luke Mitchell's son, Abe, rode with me until he met Sally in a saloon in San Antonio. They married soon afterwards and settled down on the Crazy M. They had a daughter. But soon after that, fever swept the ranch and claimed the lives of Sally and Luke. Abe was heartbroken, but he was still a young man. Instead of running wild like I had done when my pa died, Abe began to build the

Crazy M into the ranch it is now. Some years later he remarried and changed the ranch's name to the Double M.'

'Why? asked Jane.

'Abe's second wife had also been married before and had a young son. Her name was Ann Miller. The son from her first marriage was Brad whom Abe regards as his son. The old man now takes a back seat and in effect Brad runs the Double M.'

Jane was so taken aback by the ranger's revelation, she could hardly breathe. Brad would one day inherit the Double M. Little wonder he had more money than the average cowboy. And that also explained why he had followed the renegades across New Mexico, but not why a Texas Ranger had also tracked the outlaws.

'Ethan, what was your real reason for coming to Blackwater?'

'To protect Brad.'

'How come?'

'After the San Pedro massacre, Abe Mitchell contacted my captain and asked him to send someone after Brad. I was working near the New Mexican border and knowing my connection with Abe, my captain gave me leave of absence.'

'But how did you know where Brad was going?' asked Jane.

'The Texas Rangers had already received information that Killner's gang were intending to set up
a new base in a mining camp near Blackwater. I
rode directly to it, only to find that neither they
nor Brad had arrived. So I hung around the
mining camp waiting for something to happen.
You could have knocked me down with a feather
when I rode into the Little U with Dorrell and
discovered Brad working as your hired hand.'

The return of Brad ended the discussion. It was
now his turn to ride with Jane.

Mounted on Jane's little pinto, but using his
own saddle, Ethan guided the wagon into the
wastelands. In the far distance, a plume of black
smoke rose high into the blue sky. It came from
the direction of the mining camp. But in spite of
their curiosity, Ethan decided it was not safe to
investigate its cause in broad daylight.

Instead, the ranger led them to a relatively safe
place to camp. By chance, he had stumbled on the
site during his travels to and from the mine. It was
little more than a shallow crater, but although
waterless, it was almost completely surrounded by
tree-tall cacti. Nevertheless, Ethan deemed it was
not safe to light a fire, so they had to make do with
cold beans and water from their canteens.
Illuminated by the light of the full moon, they ate
a Spartan meal. As they did so, Ethan began to talk

130

about the white man Jane had shot.

'Some customs of the Indians are hard to understand,' he said. 'They probably massacred his folks when he was little more than a baby. Yet they brought the boy up as one of their own. So he became a real Apache in everything except appearance.'

But that was little consolation to Jane. A white 'Indian' he may have been, but he was still a man. She detested violence in all its forms. Indeed, even when she had needed food, she had never killed any of her hens. Yet, this day, a man was dead by her own hand. As she shivered at the thought, Brad put a protective arm around her shoulder. She shivered again, so it seemed only natural that Brad should hold her a little tighter.

Sensing his presence was not needed, Ethan decided to investigate the fire coming from the mining camp. To do this, he needed something a little larger than Jane's little pinto, so he borrowed Prince and then rode slowly out of the camp.

Even when Jane had stopped shivering, Brad's arm remained around her shoulder. She made no effort to pull away.

'I guess I'm in your debt again. I haven't thanked you yet for saving my life,' he said.

'Somebody has to look after you.'

'Long may it be you,' he replied, and kissed her tenderly.

She returned the kiss with interest and then snuggled closer into him.

CHAPTER THIRTEEN

Disturbed by his arrival, buzzards rose into the light blue sky, then circled overhead. Their discordant calls filled the air as they seemed to be waiting for his departure. Only then could they return to feast on the carcasses of the dead. Yet there were no miners in the camp. Nor were there any guards and the corral was empty, its unlatched gate swinging idly in the dawn breeze.

Amazed, Ethan could only survey the scene of utter devastation which lay before him. He drew and cocked his old Griswold & Gunnison and examined its octagonal barrel carefully. There must be no misfires this time. Only when he was fully satisfied did he urge Prince slowly forward into the heart of the mining camp. As he did so, the early morning sun glinted on the gun's polished brass frame.

The main eating hall had been completely destroyed. Yet row after row of the big white tents used by the miners were undamaged. However, they were all empty.

So where were the miners? Having spent all their hard-earned money in the Lucky Strike saloon, by now most should have returned from Blackwater. Even at this early hour, the campsite should have be buzzing with life as the miners prepared themselves for work. Although there were a multitude of wagon tracks leading to and from the camp, there was no sign of life. Apart from the buzzards still wheeling overhead, it was eerily quiet.

The reason was not hard to find. As he rode out of the camp and approached the actual mine, it was clear that it had been dynamited. The blast had caused a major landslide on the slopes above the mine with devastating results. Thousands of tons of rock had cascaded down the hillside and then crashed down on the mine's entrance, completely sealing it. The devastation was on such a vast scale, it didn't need an expert to work out that the Blackwash mine would never be worked again.

The blast must have been heard for miles, yet the ranger had heard nothing. Nor had Brad or Jane reported hearing anything while they had been on the ridge watching over the Barr Zero herd. So Ethan concluded the blast must have occurred while they were in the cave, fighting the Apaches.

The smoke he had seen yesterday must have come from the burnt-out buildings by the mine shaft. The bodies of the clerks still lay where they had been shot and already showed the grizzly effects of the buzzards.

The ranger carefully surveyed the chaos. None of the dead men had been armed. The scene was so disturbingly reminiscent of the San Pedro massacre, he had little doubt it was the handiwork of Killner's gang.

Yet there was no sign of the magnificent stage-coach, nor of the six snow-white horses used to pull it. Did that mean Hawker had left before the raid had begun? But if that was the case, what had happened to the gunmen he paid to guard the mine? Had they fled without fighting? That seemed unlikely, but if they had, Brad and Jane might be in danger. Unsurprisingly, the idea that Hawker would leave the Blackwash mine unguarded and send all his gunmen to take over the Little U never occurred to him.

There was nothing more to be gained by staying in the mining camp. Reluctantly leaving the dead bodies to the buzzards, he turned Prince round and then made his way back. As he did so, he scoured the ground for tracks, but, of course, there was none and his return to his companions was uneventful. Over another cold meal, he related to Brad and Jane what he had seen.

'Do you think it was the work of Kiliner's gang?' asked Brad.

'Can't be absolutely sure, but it sure looks like their handiwork,' he replied.

'Then we are not safe out here,' said Brad looking hard at Jane. 'I guess we had better head for Blackwater.'

'You're right,' agreed the ranger. 'Perhaps Marshal Ward might know what's been happening.'

'But what about Dent?' asked Jane. 'I thought he was supposed to be the sheriff of the mining camp. And where is Chad Dorrell and the camp's gunmen?'

Ethan still had no answers and just shook his head in bewilderment. He had no way of knowing that Dent was already dead. Nor could he know the mine's gunmen were about to become expendable pawns. Their presence at the Little U was intended to provoke a bitter response from the Barr Zero, a reaction which Hawker intended to turn into a full-blooded range war.

Kayleigh Barr was not exaggerating when she

had told Brad that nothing went on in Blackwash County without Hawker's knowledge and approval. Investigating the cause of the explosion, her scouts had located the missing herd of cattle and they had discovered that the Little U was full of Hawker's gunmen.

This occupation was intended to be permanent. However, a dozen gunmen take a lot of feeding. So, as dawn broke, Chad Dorrell set out for Blackwater. His purpose, to arrange for a continuous stream of food and ammunition from Hawker's store and a generous supply of whiskey from the Lucky Strike.

However, as Hawker intended, the occupation of the Little U by his gunmen was all the excuse Kayleigh Barr needed to attack the Little U. As the ranger returned to the campsite, her men swooped down on the small ranch.

But Hawker had failed to foresee that Chad Dorrell would not stay with his men. Without his leadership, the gunmen had become careless and thinking they were safe from attack, no guards had been posted. So, when the Barr Zero attacked, most of the gunmen were caught out in the open completing their ablutions.

Nevertheless, they were all professional gunfighters and the Barr Zero cowhands were not. After the initial setback, during which two gunmen were killed and another badly wounded, those who had remained in the ranch house laid down a deadly hail of bullets. Under its cover, the rest of the gunmen made it back to of the ranch house.

Still mounted, the Barr Zero hands again charged the Little U ranch house. For some, it was the last thing they did. Hawker's gunmen held their fire until the last possible moment and then opened fire. At point-blank range, they couldn't miss. No less than five Barr Zero men crashed from their saddles never to rise again. But it wasn't enough to turn the tide in favour of the gunmen.

Nevertheless, shocked by the number of fatalities, Kayleigh signalled her men to withdraw, but another ranch hand was hit fatally before the rest of the Barr Zero men rode out of range. In all, six ranch hands had been killed, one was badly injured, and another two had received minor flesh wounds. In spite of the losses, the Barr Zero ranch hands still heavily outnumbered Hawker's gunmen. Kayleigh realized though that the fire power from the ranch house was too deadly for the Little U to be taken by storm.

Yet there was no need. She counted that it was a hundred paces from the ranch house to the corral which had been repaired since her last visit. Also, top rails had been added to all its sides. The gunmen's horses were all in the corral and had been unsaddled. Therefore, Hawker's men were trapped in the house.

Kayleigh ordered her men to dismount. While most of them laid down covering fire, the remainder raced to the barn. They reached the barn safely and swiftly disappeared inside. From the safety of its hayloft, they overlooked the corral gate and had a clear shot at anyone trying to use it, with little fear of being hit by return fire. She then ordered the rest of the hands to encircle the ranch house.

For several hours nothing happened. But then the door was flung open and two gunmen made a dash for the corral. The rest laid down volley after volley in a vain attempt to cover them. But it had no effect on the men in the barn's hayloft who waited until the two gunmen had opened the corral gate before they opened fire.

Both gunmen fell to the ground, never to rise again. But to the dismay of the gunmen in the ranch house, the shots spooked the horses and they bolted out of the corral's open gate and galloped away.

'I don't think they will try that again,' said Kayleigh.

Her informants had told her that Jane had visited Blackwater to purchase food and supplies. Clearly, she had not returned to the Little U, so

Kayleigh correctly deduced that the ranch house did not contain enough food to sustain Hawker's gunmen for more than a few days. Therefore, all she had to do was to stay put and starve the gunmen out.

However, patience was not one of Kayleigh Barr's virtues. She issued another order and a rider was dispatched to the Barr Zero. Kayleigh watched him ride away. It would be some hours before he would be able to return with a wagon loaded with bundles of hay and a barrel of lamp oil. If she could not take the ranch house by storm she would burn it down, thus forcing Hawker's men into the open where they would receive no mercy.

Apart from dealing Hawker and his Blackwash mine a crippling blow, she would finally resolve the problem of the Little U. But it was not the ranch house she wanted; it was the extra water in the one green valley in the Cactus Hills.

Well out of range of Hawker's men, Kayleigh settled down by the stream and watched the hens as they scurried for insects. There would be plenty of eggs for breakfast, but not for Hawker's gunmen.

CHAPTER FOURTEEN

They were still some distance away from Blackwater when Brad suddenly reined in Prince. The ground in front of his horse had become soft enough to reveal the imprint of several recently made horse tracks. Among them were the prints of a horseshoe with a v-shaped pattern cut into it.

The ranger, once again incongruously mounted on Jane's little pinto, pulled up beside him.

'I followed those right across New Mexico,' Brad said, as he pointed to the tracks. 'I guess Killner's gang are already in Blackwater.'

Jane drew level with them and pulled up her old wagon. The cart-horse towered over the ranger mounted on the little pinto.

'Anything wrong?' she asked.

'No,' lied the ranger. 'But it seems we may have some unfinished business to settle rather sooner than we thought. Is there anyone you could stay with while we check out Blackwater?'

'I could stay with my friend, Alice Albright; she has a house just out of town.'

The name caused Brad to recall his first visit to Blackwater and his conversation with Marshal Ward. He needed answers, but there was the little matter of Killner's gang to tackle before he could plan for the future. So he said nothing.

Unaware of the violent events in Blackwater, Jane had expected Alice to be in the Lucky Strike supervising her girls. So she had little fear of Brad uncovering the secrets of her past. However, as they approached Alice's surprisingly well-appointed house, its owner rushed out to greet her. To Jane's dismay, her former boss was followed by several girls whose saucy attire left no doubt they were saloon girls. And some of them greeted Jane like a long lost friend, as indeed, she was.

While Ethan was taken aback by the bawdy nature of their reception, Brad seemed to take it all in his stride. Once he had satisfied himself that Jane would be able to stay, he kissed her and, ignoring the ribald comments from the other girls, remounted and followed Ethan to Blackwater.

As they passed the marker post which denoted

the town's limit, Brad noticed that the offices of the Overland stage had been boarded up. Yet along Main Street nothing stirred. He brought Prince to a halt. Apart from the sound of a piano playing from inside the Lucky Strike, it was suspiciously quiet. The tune seemed to be the only one the pianist knew, for as soon as he had finished, he started playing it all over again.

Brad was about to ride on when he felt the restraining arm of the ranger, who shook his head, then turned Jane's pony towards the saloon. He dismounted and Brad did the same.

At that moment, several gunmen appeared at the far end of Main Street. They had been lying low in the offices of the New Mexico Stage and Freight. In spite of the distance, the ranger recognized them instantly. They were the outlaws. Killner, though, was not amongst them.

They opened fire but the range was too great for a six-gun. So their bullets struck the ground well short of their intended targets. Prince was used to the sound of gunfire so ignored it. Not so Jane's diminutive pinto, which bolted down Main Street and did not stop until it had returned to the safety of Alice's house.

Meanwhile, the gang ran towards the Lucky Strike. Brad and the Ranger simultaneously hurled themselves through the saloon's swinging doors as the renegades again opened fire.

Brad staggered to his feet and looked for cover. There was none. The saloon's bar was deserted except for Marshal Ward who, armed with Clem Mullet's sawn-off, doubled-barrelled shotgun, was standing over the pianist forcing the terrified man to play the tune over and over again. As soon as Brad and Ethan made their somewhat undignified entrance, he allowed the pianist to stop.

'Glad you got my message,' said the marshal.

'What message?' asked Brad.

Before he could answer, the pianist suddenly stood up and rushed passed the still rising ranger. He did not stop running until he reached the middle of Main Street. Flapping his hands wildly, he began screaming at the top of his voice.

'Don't shoot! Don't shoot! It's me, Harry, the pianist. I work for Mr Hawker.'

Unfortunately for Harry, the gunmen were now in range. Nevertheless, they heeded his plea and stopped shooting, but not until the hapless pianist lay riddled with bullets on the sidewalk, a few paces from the saloon.

'We can't hold out in the bar, so follow me,' ordered Marshal Ward, as he stepped behind the bar and into a short passageway. Brad and Ethan followed. The passage led to Clem Mullet's office. There were no windows. The office was lit by a solitary oil lamp which sat in the middle of a large oak desk. Behind it was an armchair and behind the armchair was a massive bookcase which stretched from floor to ceiling.

'What now?' asked Ethan, worried they would be trapped inside the office when the outlaws attacked.

' I'll show you. But first close the door and then lock it,' replied Marshal Ward.

As soon as Ethan had completed the simple task, Blackwater's law officer pressed a button on Clem's desk. But nothing happened. Then, after picking up the oil lamp, the marshal walked over to the bookcase and removed two books. Except they weren't books, just hollow cases. Behind them was a lever, which he pulled sharply. The bookcase swung open to reveal a flight of stairs.

'The main office door has to be locked and then the catch on the desk released before the bookcase can be opened,' explained the mMarshal.

Pausing only to shut the bookcase behind them, the law officer led the way down the stairs and into another passageway. This one was shored up by ancient-looking timbers. Never a lover of enclosed spaces, Brad was glad when they reached another flight of stairs. These led upwards into the storage room of the main stores.

Marshal Ward blew out the lamp, then led them

through the store into Main Street. The outlaws were so busy preparing to storm the saloon, they failed to notice the trio as they crossed Main Street. As they approached the jailhouse, Brad could see that all its windows were shuttered as if prepared to withstand a siege. Then the marshal called out softly.

'Open up, Matt. I'm coming in and I've got two men with me.'

The jailhouse door opened. As soon as they were inside, Matt Gillard closed and bolted it.

'Matt, how's our prisoner?' asked the marshal.

'Not so chipper, after our little chat,' chuckled the smithy.

Over a mug of coffee, Marshal Ward explained.

'After I arrested Clem Mullet, Matt and I had a little chat about how hard life could be for any prisoner who withheld information from me. After that, he was most forthcoming. Hawker is the real owner of the Lucky Strike. Then Mullet admitted that without Hawker's knowledge, he had been rigging the gambling tables. He kept one set of account books to show his boss and another set which showed the extra takings.'

'Why would he do that?' asked Brad.

'Dent was Mullett's partner. It seems the sheriff didn't trust his partner and insisted he kept accurate records of the saloon's takings. After he had

146

checked the books, he helped Mullet smuggle the extra money out of the Lucky Strike by the old mine shaft.'

'So where is Dent?'

'Boot Hill. I finally found my nerve and outdrew him.'

'I thought you said he was quicker on the draw than you?'

'But not smarter,' said Blackwater's law officer as he drew his short-barrelled, Sheriff's Model, Peacemaker.

'Well I'll eat a mule's hind leg!' exclaimed Ethan.

'Whatever will Sam Colt's men come up with next?' asked Brad.

The ranger smiled knowingly, but instead of answering the question, asked the marshal one of his own.

'What about Kiliner's gang?'

'They robbed the bank yesterday and burnt it to the ground although I managed to get one of them before the rest got away. But they returned this morning while I was in the Lucky Strike trying to find evidence to corroborate Mullet's story. I was wondering how to tackle them when I saw you riding up Main Street, so I arranged for the pianist to send you a signal.'

'Signal? I don't understand,' said Brad.

'The tune,' said the ranger. 'It was the Deguello. It's a bugle call meaning no quarter will be given. It originated in Old Spain, but the Mexicans played it non-stop to our boys during the siege of the Alamo until they overran the mission and killed everyone inside it.'

'I didn't know if you could recognize a bugle call played on the piano,' said the marshal.

'I was four when Santa Anna and his soldiers surrounded the Alamo. We were just passing through, but Pa stayed to fight. As Ma drove us out of the Alamo, the Mexicans began to play the Deguello. It seems like a lifetime ago, but I never forgot the tune or its meaning. So when I heard the pianist playing it over and over again I took it to mean Killner's gang had laid siege to Blackwater.'

The discussion was interrupted by a heavy thud as something struck the jail door. It was followed by a shout from the opposite side of Main Street.

'Marshal! My name's Killner. I believe you have that turncoat, Ethan Madden, with you.'

'I'm right here Nate. What do you want?'

'Madden! Nobody walks out of my gang and lives, as your cousin and his friends found out in San Pedro. Tomorrow, at ten, I will start out from the New Mexico office. If you're not on the street to face me, my men will burn down Blackwater,

148

building by building.'

'I'll be there, Nate. You can count on it.'

'I wonder why Killner chose ten and not dawn?' asked the marshal, after the renegade leader had departed.

'I don't trust that back-shooter. If you go, I think you will be walking into a trap,' said Brad.

'Maybe so, but two can play that game. With your help, Marshal Ward, I have a plan which might just rid this town of the killers,' said the ranger.

Just after midnight, the marshal, who had exchanged clothes with Clem Mullet, crept out of the jailhouse. When he was certain Main Street was safe, he signalled to Brad to follow him. Silently as ghosts, they made their way down the street and entered the Lucky Strike. But that was not their destination.

Next morning, Blackwater was like a ghost town. Using the prairie schooners, the miners had left for Tombstone. The continued presence of the gang had caused most of Blackwater's residents to flee. Even the news of the shootout had not persuaded the few who had remained to leave the safety of their well-barricaded homes.

True to his word, at ten precisely, Nate Killner stepped on to the street. But he was not alone; Chad Dorrell followed him. Killner was well satisfied with his morning's work. Since dawn, his men had been in place; three in the general store and two at the back of the jail.

'Marshal, lock the door behind me,' Ethan said loudly enough for Killner to hear.

The ranger began to walk towards the two gunmen, who stood waiting for him. However, after carefully calculating the distance between them, the ranger halted. As he did so, the muffled sound of gunshots, followed by the unmistakeable blast of a shotgun, came from inside the jail.

'That's my men taking care of Marshal Ward and, as you can see, I've got my new partner with me to take care of you,' gloated Killner.

'I thought you might have that loudmouthed bum from the Little U with you,' said Dorrell.

'Said he had more important things to deal with,' Ethan replied.

'Too bad. It's hardly fair, but I guess that means you have to face the two of us,' said Dorrell.

'You're right: it's not fair. But I'm willing to wait while you get the rest of your men to even things up.'

Killner smiled at this retort. However, his expression swiftly changed as the jailhouse door opened to reveal Matt Gillard. The burly blacksmith had Clem Mullet's sawn-off shotgun in his hands and both barrels were still smoking.

'Mullet's dead. Seems the gunmen mistook him for the marshal. But they won't be making any more mistakes like that again. I blasted them with Clem's shotgun,' bellowed the burly blacksmith, loud enough for the rest of Blackwater to hear.

Killner read the situation swiftly. The loss of his men was not critical. The ultra-short barrel of the blacksmith's shotgun rendered it virtually useless in the open street, so his plan could still work. He called out to his men who had taken possession of the general store.

Immediately, Reb Rosin, followed by two other members of the gang, walked out of the general stores. But although they were approaching the ranger's back, they posed no threat to him. They were unarmed and their hands were held high above their heads.

The reason was soon clear. Behind them came Marshal Ward, wearing Clem Mullet's coat and brandishing his Sheriff's Model Peacemaker. Side by side with the marshal was Brad, toting a more orthodox Colt. Pinned to his chest was a deputy's badge. They had used the old mine shaft to get from the Lucky Strike to the general stores and were already in position when the renegades entered the store. The rest was relatively easy.

'Killner, you've made a fine mess of this,' snarled Dorrell.

'Not a bit of it,' he replied. 'From the moment we left San Pedro, I planned for this showdown with Madden. I left so many clues along the trail for him to follow, he couldn't help but find me.'

'What about the marshal and his new deputy?' asked Dorrell.

'They can't shoot us from the general store and after we've dealt with the ranger, the marshal's mine,' retorted Killner as he went for his six-gun.

Even without the aid of Dorrell, Killner knew he was too quick for Madden. And so it proved. His six-gun spat lead before the ranger's gun had left its holster. Dorrell, even faster, also outdrew the lawman. His pearl-handled six-guns usually spat messages of death. But not this time. Like those of Killner, its bullets struck the ground a couple of inches in front of the ranger's boots. His calculations had proved to be exactly right.

Ethan Madden's draw was slow but he still managed to fire twice. But it was not his old brass-framed Griswold and Gunnison, but the gun he had been keeping in his cavalry-style holster.

Surprisingly, its bullets reached their target. The first hit Killner in the chest, penetrated his heart and killed him instantly. The second struck Dorrell in the shoulder. The force of its impact sent the gunman reeling. As he staggered to his feet, he transferred his Colt to his left hand.

'Drop your gun. You haven't a chance; my Colt outranges yours,' said the ranger.

'You're bluffing,' responded Dorrell.

As two more shots rang out. A look of bewilderment spread over Dorrell's face. His bullet had again fallen short, but pain burnt through his chest. A crimson tide of blood began to pour down his fancy black shirt. Surprisingly, he was still standing and felt no pain. But his Colt began to feel very heavy. So heavy, he had to let it drop to the ground. Seconds later, he slumped down and was dead by the time Ethan reached him, never knowing the instrument of his death.

The ranger holstered his new Colt Peacemaker. But this one had a specially adapted, extra long, barrel, giving it a better range. Specially produced for the Texas Rangers, in later years it was to become known as the Buntline Special.

EPILOGUE

It was almost noon. Although a day had passed since the shootout, Jane had not seen Brad. Nor did she expect to do so again. By now, he must have found out about her past and the heir to one of the largest and most wealthy ranches in Texas was not about to continue a serious relationship with a former saloon girl. But Brad was not her only loss.

She looked at the still smouldering ruins of the Little U. With tears in her eyes, she stumbled up to what was left of the ranch house. Distraught, she turned towards the barn, only to find it was nothing more than a burnt-out shell.

Everything for which she had worked so hard to build up had been destroyed, leaving Jane with little more than the clothes she was wearing. She

154

sank to the ground and burst into a flood of bitter tears.

How long she cried, she couldn't tell. But the tears eventually stopped and she began to plan. After the death of her father, hadn't she rebuilt the Little U? To get the money she had needed, she had 'entertained' the miners. And hadn't she been one of the most sought-after saloon girls in Blackwater? She had done it once and would do it again. Even if the miners had gone, there would still be plenty of ranch hands willing to pay for entertainment.

For that purpose, Alice would give her a room in her house and when the Lucky Strike reopened, she would again become its principal singer. Her singing voice was of little importance as long as she was prepared to show her legs and perhaps a little more. She had lost Brad, so what did it matter?

Lost in her plans for the future, she barely noticed the passing of time. But the arrival of her old wagon broke her trance. To her surprise, the driver was Brad. His horse, Prince, trotted obediently behind the old wagon in the way that only a Missouri Fox-Trotter can. She rose and forced a smile. But his face remained grim.

'What a mess. I'm afraid there's nothing left. What will you do now?' he said.

'Go home. I guess you know where I belong,'

she replied. Of course she meant Alice's house of ill repute, although she could not bring herself to say so.

'I guess I do. Will you let me drive you there?'

So she had lost him. She couldn't look him in the face for fear of the disapproval she would see there.

'Yes. It's much too far to walk,' she replied mechanically.

'It sure is,' he replied as he helped her into the wagon.

As soon as it started to move, exhaustion swept over her. Without realizing it, she had watched over the dying embers of the Little U for hours and although she tried to stay awake, she could not.

Sensing her exhaustion, Brad transferred the reins to his right hand, and put his left arm around her shoulders. She snuggled up to him, and then fell into a deep sleep. Until they reached Alice's house, she could at least dream that he was still her man.

But hours later when she woke up, they were nowhere near Blackwater. It was dusk and she was alone in the back of her old wagon. For an instant she panicked, but the smell of hot coffee and roasting meat not only reassured her, but made her realize just how long it was since she had eaten.

More than a little stiff, she climbed awkwardly out of the wagon. It seemed that Brad had unhitched the cart-horse while she slept, for he was tethered by Prince. Brad was sitting by a roaring fire over which he had suspended a huge joint of beef. A boiling coffee pot was perched by the side of the fire.

'What are we doing here?' she asked.

'Waiting for Ethan. In this part of New Mexico they dispense rough justice. The bank robbers were tried this morning while you were at the Little U. They were found guilty and by now hanged. Ethan stayed to give Marshal Ward a hand to organize things.'

Jane shuddered at the thought of the hanging. It was rough justice, to be sure. But if only a half of what she had heard about them was true, no more than they deserved.

'Then, after the hanging, there's going to be a presentation. The good folk of Blackwater have donated enough money to buy a good horse to replace the one the ranger lost to the Apaches, so I expect he will join us before sun-up.'

Jane's thoughts reverted to her present situation.

'Where are we?' she asked.

'Enough questions. Eat now and talk later,' said Brad slicing a huge wedge of meat from the underside of the still roasting beef.

She needed no second bidding for she was starving. As she ate, Brad poured out a large mug of coffee and gave it to her. It was very hot, too strong and very sweet. Nevertheless, he had to refill her mug twice before she had had enough. Although she had to use her bare hands, she devoured all the beef on her plate.

'Sorry, I forgot to bring any forks,' he apologized.

By the time she had finished it was night and the moon had begun to rise.

'Where are we going?' she demanded.

'Home,' he replied evasively.

'No we're not, Brad Miller, I know all the trails between the Little U and Blackwater. This isn't one of them, so where are you taking me?'

Her heart skipped a beat as he smiled at her.

'To the Double M. You said I could take you home, so that's where we're going.'